ALAN KELLY was born in Bellshill in 19(North Lanarkshire. At sixteen, he started work as a labourer with North Lanarkshire Council Roads Department where he was to spend the next twenty years road-sweeping, litter-picking and drain-cleaning; he was eventually promoted to a tar squad, specialising in 'skills' such as tar-shovelling, tar-raking, tar-chipping and tar-rolling. Around this time he married, but he was losing his battle against alcoholism and he and Patricia divorced four years later. Then a chance meeting with an old friend, Des Dillon, changed the course of his life. Des, who was running a local writers' group, encouraged him to join and put his experiences down on paper. Tarmen's yarns heard from legendary local storytellers were the inspiration for short stories, some of which were published in *Cutting Teeth* magazine. They also form the basis of *The Tar Factory,* his first novel. Although all of the characters in this book are fictional, *The Tar Factory* is hardwired into the authentic experience of generations of tarmen who used black humour and macho-man storytelling as a survival mechanism.

Alan now works as a school janitor. He's been sober for eleven years and lives in Airdrie with Patricia – they re-married in 1995 – and their little dog, Mollie the Collie.

The Tar Factory

ALAN KELLY

Luath Press Limited

EDINBURGH

www.luath.co.uk

First published 2004

The author's right to be identified as author of this book
under the Copyright, Designs and Patents Act 1988 has been asserted.

The paper used in this book is neutral-sized and recyclable.
It is made from elemental chlorine free pulps
sourced from renewable forests.

Printed and bound by
DigiSource GB Ltd, Livingston

Typeset in 10.5 point Sabon

To my wife Patricia,
for giving me a second chance

Chapter One.
The beginning or the end?
Take yer pick.

Mad Dog's in jail.
The party's over, man.
The Crazy Gang no more.

Finished. Fuckin finished so we are. The game's a bogey.

Been here twenty years now. Twenty summers.

Bastart.

Down the fuckin swanny, just like that.
A job for life! A job for life, they said.
Aye, son, a rock-steady job. Rock-steady Eddy. Steady as a
teetotaller on a tight-rope tossin chainsaws.

Good pension. Sick pay. Holidays galore.
Be a good boy son. Be here forever.
Head down arse up keep yer nose clean.

A job for life, son. Aye.

An now it's all over. It's time for the fat burd to sing.

Listen.

The big Mamma's countin the beat.
Snappin her fingers. Tappin her feet.

Mad Dog's in jail.
Mad Dog's a dead, man. Well, not yet. But he soon will be.
Aw, for fuck sake. Big Mad Dog.

Chapter Two.
Blaw Knox.

Ah wondered why the fuck they called him Mad Dog.
Hey listen. Ah wasn't long in findin out.

Wait till ah tell ye this.

It was ma very first shift.
This big baw-heided cunt walks in. Superintendent Brown was
his name.
They dubbed him Big Hovis.
Remember the advert on the telly? Don't say Brown, say Hovis.

That was it, man. It fuckin stuck. Stuck like a non-stick fryin
pan.
Nicknames stick, man. Watch out, bro. Watch you don't get
a nickname.

Hovis told me to go with Blaw Knox.
Blaw Knox, who the fuck's Blaw Knox?
Ye know what it's like, man, ye try to get a picture.
Blaw Knox?
OK. Ye're lookin for some beer-bellied sweaty cunt with a
ten-day growth an his hairy arse crack hangin out the jeans.

Check that arse crack, man. An that one over there. An that
one. An that one. Fuck me, man. They're everywhere ye look,
so they are.
Ah'm tellin ye, it was like a fuckin cracks-of-arses-hangin-out-
of-jeans convention. Ye could park a motorbike in some of
their arses.
Hey, park yer motorbike here, boy. Harley Davidson?
No problem.

Blaw Knox? Fuck. Could be any cunt.

Cagey. Play it cagey. Ye know what it's like when yer new,
don't ye. Always got to be on yer guard, so ye have. Watch out
for wind-ups.
Say nothin. Fuck all. Keep the mouth shut.
Thank Christ ah did too.
Wait till ah tell ye this.

We're out on the job. Hi-tec tarlayin.

These big lorry loads of black stuff start emptyin their bowels
into the jaws of the Big Green Mean Machine.
She opens her mighty jaws wide gulpin down big mouthfuls.
No fuckin bother, man. Ye want to see this. Big lumps of
steamy hot tar gettin munched an crunched into tiny wee
pieces an oozin out her arse in a fluffy fine powder. Sizzlin hot.
Steamy n black.

Along comes the chipper givin a rhythmic clickety click an
sprayin it with pre-coated chips that shine like a billion
beetles.
An then along comes Big Bertha, the red-hot steam roller.
Twenty tonnes of girth huffs an puffs an clunks an clanks an
farts big steam balls out her arse.
She's chasin the chipper, rollin in those chips. Pressin the tarry
mat flat.
Aye, that's a tarman term. The mat. Nice shiny flat mat. Press it
flat, man. Shiny flat mat. Flat as a gymnast's tit.
It just caught the edge of my eye an

WOOOOOOOOMMMF

It hit me like a blooter on the back of the neck with a
baseball bat.

Aye, it just fuckin hit me like that, man.
There it was, by the way. Right on the side of the tar machine
in big yellow letters the size of a Rottweiler's head

BLAW KNOX MASTER ROADLAYER/PAVER

Aw, man, ah would've fuckin died. Imagine it, can you fuckin
well imagine it?
Walkin up an right in front of every cunt goin, Eh, I'm lookin
for Blaw Knox. What one of you cunts is Blaw Knox?

Jesus Christ, man. See what ah'm sayin? Cagey cagey. Watch
out for wind-ups. Yer better off sayin nothin. Aye, yer better
off sayin fuck-all.

Anyway, where was ah? Aye.
Big Mad Dog, man. The first time ah saw him.
Ah'll never forget it, by the way.
Aye, he was standin over there.
Big icy blue eyes, starin. Trapped in a trance. Solid gone, man.
Gone with the wind.
Mad Dog. Fuckin Mad.

He was eyeballin the wheel on the side of the roller. The
brilliant shiny bright cuttin wheel shavin a baw hair off the
edge of the mat, givin that nice polished finish.

SIllllllliiiiiiiiiiissss   she goes

like the world's biggest pizza cutter slicin through hot bubbly
cheese.

Crazy D said somethin that started the whole thing off.
Aye, Crazy D planted the seed.
Imagine that thing goin through yer leg, he said. Ye wouldn't
feel a thing, man. Happened to one of my best mates, so it did.

Felt fuck-all. Nothin.
Took his leg clean off in less than a tenth of a second.
Fuck ye, man.

Zeeeeeeep

Whipped it off just like that.
Cut cleaner than a deck of cards.
Forty gran he got. Forty fuckin gran an a pension.

Mad Dog's ears lit up like a freshly kennelt fire. His eyeballs
popped out their sockets. The big cunt would put his granny's
arse on the street for a tenner.
Into anythin bar a nun's knickers.
Hold it. Change that last bit.

Fuck-all wrong with a nun's knickers, he'd say.

So anyway, he starts rantin an ravin.
Forty fuckin G's. Forty fuckin smackeroos. Aw, the name-a-
fuck, man, set ye up for life so it would. No worries. Fuckin
easy street.

Just think, forty big ones in the bank. An remember yer man
here's got twenty years service. Yer lookin at a hundred an
forty notes a week, easy. Stroll on, eh? Just think, pay yer
house off, take the weans a cruise, buy them bikes, computers
an all yer fancy clobber. Y'know the stuff ah'm talking about,
all that fancy named stuff?

An her? Imagine her. Over the fuckin moon, she'd be. Fitted
lavvy fitted kitchen fancy leather suite an mirrored wardrobes.
Aw, man. Fuck.

An what about that big Shogun too. Aye, always fancied a
Shogun. Cruisin through the streets, man. Cool dude cruisin.

Wearin the dark shades.
Aye, just press a button an roll down the window, hangin the
arm out givin cunts the finger. Fuckin up yees. Easy street.

Fuckin doddle, man. No pain. Mad Dog don't feel pain. Pain's
for pussies. Big wheel cuts so fine. Painless.

Feel the pain later. So what? Who gives a fuckin shit, man?
Later don't count. Fuck what happens later.

It's perfect too. Here. Right here right now. Right in the middle
of the main street. Fuckin place is jumpin. Hundred an one
witnesses. Check up there. Look. CCTV. Big Brother's watchin
ye, man. Smile, yer on Candid Camera.
Mad Dog jumps up an down. What's he like, eh? Doin the
war dance.
Aye, doin the Mad Dog dance. Fuckin punchin the air. One
two, one two. Up on the tiptoes, does a birly then leaps
through the air throwin kung fu kicks.

Yesssssssssssssssssssssssssssssssssssss.

This is how it goes, Mad Dog tells D. Here's the script.
Yer just drivin yer roller as normal, right? Yer cuttin away
focusin like fuck down there on the auld guide bar. Beady eyes
fixed. Ye don't look back. The golden rule. A good roller man
never looks back. Focus focus focus. Don't even blink. We're
talkin precision here. We're talkin midges' pubes, right. No
room for error. So yer lookin nowhere but down.
Down there at the shiny wheel.
Yer fuckin tranced.

Mad Dog rolls a fag. Lums up, sucks in hard an blows out.
Now yer man here, he says, drummin the chunky thumb into
the chest.

Ah'll be round the other side with the auld head down arse up
graftin away as usual, right. Busy busy bee. Next thing ah
know ah'm in a Turkish bath. All this fuckin steam. Ah'm
trapped, man, ah'm blind. Can't see ma fuckin hooter. All ah'll
be able to hear is these rumblin an crunchin an sizzlin noises.
Holy Jesus, ah start to panic. Can't breathe, naw, all this heavy
sweaty shit gathers in my throat an then, CRACK, fuck ye, a
sharp jag on the knee.
Aye, that's all ah'll feel, man. A slight nip. No sharper than a
bee sting.

Listen D, Mad Dog says.
All ye'll feel is a slight jolt. Just a slight dink. An ye'll wonder
what the fuck was that, eh? Is that they fuckin weans throwin
stones under the wheels an watchin them gettin crunched flat?
Wee bastarts.
An then ye'll hear this howlin scream that'll blow yer bollocks
apart an ye'll look down an see this big bubbly blood puddle,

an waaaaaaaarrrrggghhhhh,

It's up to you from there on, he tells D. Go cuckoo. Go fuckin
potty, man. The more hysterical the better. Lay it on thick, bro.
Jump up an down, pull yer hair out, gouge out yer eyeballs,
cut yer fuckin throat, man. Do what ye like just lay it on thick.
The worse the better. C'mon, man, yer fuckin traumatised.

Aw, poor Crazy D. Check him out. He ain't so sure no more.
Starts huffin an puffin graspin at straws sayin that he wasn't
sure, just heard the story from somebody that heard it from
somebody that heard it from somebody else. Don't know for
sure, bro. Just think about it will ye, eh? Think it through.
Ah mean, ye know these stories ye hear about cunts, man. The
auld leg gets whipped off an they're lyin there months later

givin it, Aw, ma fuckin leg. They can actually still feel the auld leg givin them grief. Aye, they can still feel the twingin in the knee or the heel, numbness in the feet, itchy toes even.
Aye, they're fuckin dyin to scratch toes that ain't there. Itchy toes? What toes ya daft bastart?

Crazy D goes, Aw, goan think about it, Mad Dog.

Mad Dog goes back, OK, man, ah'll think about it.
Right, ah've thought about it. Let's go.

Perfect plannin, man. Mad Dog's in charge of the chipper.
Now it usually sprays them out nice as ye like. But sometimes it jams up an lays big clumps, right? So ye follow it up an knock them about with a shovel.
An then other times it leaves big baldy bits.
Aye, big baldy patches.

Mad Dog's back there checkin. Haw cunty, he shouts at Sid. Look at this, man, look at all these clumpy bits. Like haemorrhoids hangin out an arse, so they are. An look at all these bits in between, man, they're smoother than a Buddhist's napper.
Aye, Mad Dog's back there bawlin an shoutin at Sid.

Tense. The big guy's tight as a straight-jacket.
Here comes Bertha.
Huffin an puffin. Big balls of steam screamin out her arse.
Mad Dog disappears. He's blinded. Can't see a fuckin thing, man. Zilcho. Good, he's thinkin. Good. Me can't see them, they can't see me, eh? Simple.

D's chalk white. None too happy. Doesn't fancy it, man. Doesn't fancy it one wee bit. No choice but. None. Mad Dog's words haunt his head.

Focus focus focus. Focus on the wheel an concentrate, ya cunt. Just don't look back. A good roller driver doesn't look back.

D keeps starin. Eyeballin the guide bar. Sweat's blindin him. His pores open wider than Silky's arsehole. Aw, check D's arsehole. Goin bloat-bloat-bloat, so it is. Bloatin in an out like a frog's throat. Check the knuckles, man. Chalk white. White like Caspar's head.
Mad Dog's down on his hunkers.

Stay down, man, he's tellin hisself. Gotti keep low. Hide inside the big steam ball. We're nearly there.

All that gruntin n grindin n hissin's gettin closer. He can fuckin hear it, man. Mad Dog can hear it.

Big Bertha's breathin down his neck so close he can taste it. Its manky oily heat catches his breath an boils his tonsils. It melts his fuckin eyeballs an singes the hair on his face.
Come on ya big bastart, let's do it. Just you an me now. Go for it. No way back now. No way back.

Five feet   four feet   three   two   one

Down.

              Down we go.
                      Down.

Fourteen stone of madness crashes down to earth. Eyes tight shut, teeth grindin, head spinnin round an round like the whole wide world's about to burst.

Mad Dog feels like he's gonni pass out.

Heat, man. Just heat. That's all he feels on the side of the knee. He's scared to look down, so he is. Can't look down.

He sees it in his mind. The blade. The blade penetratin the skin, aye, slicin right through skin, muscle, cartilage, bone the lot. Right through an out the other side.

Aw, fuckin easy peezy, lads. Painless. See what ah mean? Painless.

Mad Dog feels no pain. Naw. Pain's for pussies.

There's just this burnin. A fuckin horrible burnin smell like fuck knows what. Flesh mibbe? Burnin flesh?
Naw, it's like burnin fuckin fuck knows what, man.

Brakes!!!

Aye, brakes burnin.
Brakes. Brakes. BRAKES, YA BASTART

Aaaaahhhrrrrrrrgggghhhhhhhh.

Brakes. Aye.

Mad Dog opens his eyes. Clocks the blade. The brilliant shiny blade touchin his leg. Touchin an no more. Honest to pure fuck, man, a millionth of a millimetre. Ye couldn't get a pussy hair down the space. Couldn't.
Bastart bastart bastart.
No blood no bones no nothin. Bastart.
Wait a minute. No blood no bones no money, right?
Fuckin lyin there like a tit.
All this for nothin, man, all the theatrics.

Crazy D's fuckin bottled it.
Look at him sittin there wearin the little-puppy-pissed-the-carpet look.
Bottled it. Fuckin shapt in the nest. Cunt. Pure cunt, man. Sittin there whimperin an whinin an sayin he couldn't do it.

Aw, ah couldn't do it big man. Sorry, ah'm fuckin sorry, ah'm sorry, it's just, it's just, it's just that, aw, fuck, fuck fuck fuck fuck fuck.

Mad Dog starts howlin. Howlin mad. Madder than the maddest March hare. Gonni murder D. Callin him all the bastarts.

Ya bastart ye, ya yellow-bellied bastart. Ye're a fuckin pussy, so ye are. Ye're a fuckin eunuch. Ye've got no balls no fuckin balls, ya cunt. None.
Aye, Mad Dog hated cunts with no balls.

Chapter Three.
Jam rags an Johnny bags.

Ah soon found myself stuck on the gulley motor. Aye, ah remember it well. Seems like last week.
Hovis poked his head round the corner.

The gulley motor. Who fancies a shot on the gulley motor?

Well yer new, right? Yer new an yer sittin there keen as a Cub Scout, keen as fuck to impress.

Ah'll do it. No problem, man, no problemo.

Mistake number one. Never volunteer. Never. Volunteer for fuck-all. Ye find that out at yer peril, so ye do.

Clean shite out of drains? Train a fuckin monkey, so ye could. Nothin to it, man, ye just lift the lid ram the auld tube down pull the lever an

        wheeeeeeeeeeeeeeeeeeeeekle.

Up it goes, man. Offski. All the shite's up the pipe. Tatti bye, man. Now ye see it, now ye don't. Skoosh case.

Aye, skoosh case ma arse. The things are choked to fuck, so they are. Jam-packed. Full to the brim with shit.

Not that kinda shit but. Not the kinda shit yer thinkin about, like dog shit, bird shit, weans's shit. Naw, naw, naw. Every other kinda shit in the book, you name it, it's there. Typewriters beer cans buckie bottles basins. Porn magz hanbags jam rags n Johnny bags. Aye, they're all down there, man. Down in the devil's dungeon.

See yer big pipe, by the way? Forget it. Hasn't got a look in.
Ye've got to get the sleeves up, grab the big tweezers n pull
the gummfff out. Aw, fuck me, sweaty socks n fanny pads.

Nightmare.

Another thing. Ye get no help. Naw. They tell ye fuck-all.
Nothin.
They just go, Och, it's no bother young filla, it's a dawdle. It's
only silt, so it is. Honest, ye'll get harder shite in a new
wean's nappy.

But that silt that's softer than the stuff in a new wean's nappy
dries up, doesn't it? The fuckin stuff dries up an goes hard-
baked. Harder than a stallion's champer.

No problem. Naw, no problemo, man. All ye do there is fire
some water down an soften it up a bit, sploosh it around
makin it go all slushy an easy to sook up.

Aye, no problemo if ye know what yer doin, eh?

But ye don't, do ye? Naw, ye don't, cos yer new an no cunt's
told ye.

So there's yours truly saunterin along quite the thing, man.

Up with the lid   down with the big sooker   let the lever go an
      wait   wait   wait.

                    What the fuck?

                    A heavy drumroll like thunder

then

gurgle   gurgle   gurgle   gurgle

                    splaaammaaaassssh.

Two ton of lumpy muck water hits ye square on the jaw.

Blackout.

Ye're fuckin black, man. Cola Dan.

An the stink goes right up yer hooter an down yer throat
before ye can say, Oh ya bastart ye, what the fuck was that?
What was that?

That was a blow-back. Aye, that's what that was. Forgot to tell
ye son, never drop the pipe into dry dirt, it draws all the air
out the tank an blows all the shite right back into yer face.
Hundred mile an hour stuff. Blow yer fuckin head off.

Cheers, mate, thanks for tellin me. Cunt.

It gets worse. Ye get sent out to the country among the
haystacks an wheat fields. Cows mooin an sheep baain an the
nice cool breeze blowin softly on the surface of the dung
heaps. It's OK, ye think. It's OK. No bottles or buckets or bike
wheels or bags. Naw.

Know what the problem is?

Frogs, man. Fuckin frogs. The drains are polluted with the
wee cunts.

Aw fuck, man, all these wee white eyes. Ten twenty thirty sets
of sad little please-please-please-don't-hurt-me little eyes.

Ah mean, what're ye supposed to do, eh?

Fuck it, man. Fuck it. Close the lid. Can't do it, so ah can't.
Can't kill them.
No way.

Ye've got to but. No choice. It's just a job, innit? Just a job.

Right, here goes. Shut the valves, let the pressure build. Fifty, sixty, seventy pounds. Fuck ye, that'll do it.

Whoooooooooooooooooooooooooooooooooooooooooooooooosh.

Off they go, little desperadoes splashin about fightin for their lives. Croak croak croakin, man, croakin one by one. Makin leaps for freedom with their wee throats bulgin an eyes bloatin an all sorts of bloody bits of brains spewin out their arseholes. They jump about the drain an hide in the corners tryin everythin, everythin they can, but there ain't nowhere to hide. Naw, naw, sorry little chappies, yer little green arses are out the window. Fucked. Well an truly shafted. Offski up the pipe without a paddle. Off to the dark watery grave among the mud blood an shite, leavin yours truly here feelin like a fuckin serial killer.

Bastart. Just a job but, eh?

Aye, a job that leaves yer back broke yer balls bust an yer face like a dried up reservoir.

The gulley motor. The Great Whale it says on her side.
Aye, there she blows boy.
All day long ye listen to her howl. Howlin like madness an fartin out this gut gurglin stench that digs deep into yer nostrils.

Aye, train a fuckin monkey. so ye could. Ah'm the fuckin monkey. Black-face monkey with wee white eyes.

Chapter Four.
Freeze the balls off a polar bear.

An it got worse.
The very last place on this planet ye ever want to be is on the gulley motor in the cold weather. Aw, for fuck sake.

We went to work this day an it was the coldest it had been in ten thousan years. Aw, it was cold, man. Wulliebitin cold.

Ah'll tell ye how cold it was.

The *Daily Record.* Front page. Ye want to have seen what was sprawled right across the front page. A big fluffy-arsed polar bear lyin like a fireside rug. Dead. Frozen solid.

Made no difference to Hovis. Naw. None.
Big Hovis. Big hoochter choochter Hovis. Came from the Highlans ye ken. Aye, where the men are men an the sheep keep their legs crossed.

Aw, listen by the way, we're talkin about a dry guy here. Dry. Dryer than a nun's nan-pot.
Sense of humour by-pass. Ye don't kid on with the Hovis.

Ask Big Chuck.
Big Chuck Mcfuck was givin it the pish talk one day. Thinkin he's a wise guy. Thinkin he can get on yer, man's side an make him laugh. Talkin like one of the boys. Crackin jokes about the Highlaners wearin kilts so's the sheep can't hear the zips openin, an Highlaners with sheep under each arm bein called pimps.

Big Chuck's hittin him with all that patter an then standin

there waitin for Hovis to smile an say, Good one, good one.
But naw. Nothin. No smile no frown no dirty look. Nothin.
Fuckin zilcho, man. Blank.

Next day Chucky boy's down a ditch with Hovis standin over
him goin, Dig ya bastart, dig till ah tell ye to stop. Keep diggin.

Ah'm tellin ye by the way, the big boy's dryer than a camel's
baw bag.

So anyway, the big cunt's determined we're goin out this day.

C'mon, out yees go. Get they gullies cleaned. That's what yees
are paid for, ye ken. No tae sit aboot on yer erses.

We kept showin him the paper.

Look, Glasgow Zoo, man, fuckin big polar bear lyin
spreadeagled with the tongue hangin out an the lips goin
blue. Gettin measured up to become a hat n coat.

But Hovis just shrugged an turned the bottom lip down an
told us if we saw one lyin about Coatbridge to let him ken.

Out yees get. Out.

Christ Almighty, ye want to have seen the state of these drains.
Fuckin lids were locked solid, so they were. Jack Frost had sunk
his teeth in an locked his jaws tight. Metal to metal.
No chance.

Fuck it, give it a go. Come on, go for it.
Come on come on. After three.
One two three,

heeeeeeeeeeeeeeeeeeeeeeeeeeeeeaaaave.

Aw, ma head, man. Ma head goes red n the stars start zoomin

through the sky shootin into the wee dark crannies of ma
mind turnin out the light. Blackout. Ah'm fuckin blackin out,
man an goin all dizzy n light in the mind.
Aye, the head-piece starts floatin off, then

BANG

Down it comes. Crash landin on ma neck n twistin tight on the
tip of the vertebrae. Headache, man. Heavy traffic headache.
Denzo's drivin. Denzo Doom. The bold Denzo, man. Sittin
behind the wheel rantin an ravin. Rantin an ravin about
the cold.

Aw, the cold, the cold, fuckin brutal, so it is. See this climate,
worst in the world, man. Crippled ye'll be, ah'm tellin ye.
Crippled by the time yer forty. Fuckin wheel-chair ye'll need.

But yer man here's got balls. Aye, balls the size of yer head.
Stubborn as a hunger striker. Can't let it beat me. Naw.
Imagine it. The slaggin. Mad Dog an D an Chuck Mcfuck all
laughin their dicks off.
Talkin in high-pitched poofter voices goin, Oooooooh, we
couldn't get the lids up, ooooooh, the lids were too heavy.
Oooooooh, they were stuck ever so tight.
Boo hoo hoo, nearly broke all ma nails, so ah did.

Aye, ah can see them now. Hans on the hip doin the fancy
wiggly walk. An that fuck-pig Hovis. Havin to listen to his pish.
Aye, mega pish: Where ah comfi this is summer weather, so it
is. We used tae run aboot in oor simmits. Aye, we were hardy
cunts. Ate plenty purridge.

Fuck them. Fuck them all. Come on, don't give in. Don't let the
bastarts beat ye. No way, man. Ah'll show them.
Ah smack the lid with the pinch bar, batterin all four corners

to loosen it off first. That's the game, get some heat in the bastart. Ah prise the poadjer down the grid an wedge it tight in the corner. Turn it.
That's it, turn it nice an slow, nice an slow, now pull, pull ya bastart, twist an pull twist an pull.
It's crackin. Ye can hear it grindin. It's fuckin nails down a blackboard stuff. The ice an the metal part company an the lid rises slowly out the rim like a tortoise keekin out its shell.

Ah give Denzo the whistle an tell him to bring the wagon forward. Aw, check the bold Denzo out, by the way. Yer man's on fire. What a day he's havin. Magic.
Wearin the auld happy head cos it's cold an icy an grey an damp an it's Monday an everybody's scunnert an there's no point, man, what's the fuckin point, eh? Tell me. Yer only a number, 1508818, nothin else, nothin, just a number, just a means to a fuckin end, so ye are. Terrible, terrible, absolutely murder, man. Fuckin murder Polis. Good old Denzo boy.

Nearly there. Come on, man, half an inch. Start bangin. Pullin an bangin. Bang bang bang. Head back teeth tight, pain bullets beltin through ma body. Who gives a fuck, we're nearly there.

Denzo's crawlin up towards me. Crawlin up slow. Slow. He can't be arsed. What's the fuckin point, eh? Couldn't give a toss. All the fuckin one, so it is. Ye clean the drains or ye don't. Fuck it, man, yer no better thought of.

Denzo's lookin over there. Not watchin in front. Naw. He's too busy lookin at the buildins. The bastartin black an borin buildins. Been there for ever, so they have. The cunts that built them'll be well dead, ah'm tellin ye. Lyin down the boneyard pushin up the daisies. That's where yer goin, boy, that's where we're all goin, it's the only thing that's certain.

He's closin in. The engine's heavy drumroll's beatin. Three yards, two yards, one yard from home.

All of a sudden,

POP

FUCK YE.

Right out the blue the auld lid comes away like a knob out a too-wet fanny. Aye, up ye come, ya bastart.
But see all that pullin an haulin, it's made the auld head go light, an with all that ice under yer feet ye lose yer bearins totally an the next thing ye know, yer lookin at this pair of boots in mid-air.
Floatin, so they are, big black steelies floatin in front of yer eyes. An they look familiar. Ye've seen them before somewhere.
Where but? Where?
An then there's a thud an it's yer neck hittin the deck an ye realise that those floatin black boots are yours.

Denzo hits the brakes. Gives it heavy gutty. Bang.
See that ice but, ah'm tellin ye, it would win the world's slippiest ice contest easy.
The wheels lock an do a birly. It's offski. The gulley motor's offski. Twenty ton of shit goes ice skatin.
There's yours truly lyin spreadeagled. Flat on ma face, man. Star-shaped.
Next thing all ah see is this big fuckin black rubber blob slidin towards me. Aye, big rubber wheel just slides up an goes, STOP.
Fuck ye, man, right on top of ma han.
Couldn't believe it. Ye couldn't've done it if ye tried, man,

honest to fuck. Million to one chance.
Parked its arse right there.

Ma han, aw, ma fuckin han, man, where is it where is it?
Ma han.

The brainbox doesn't fathom it, can't work it out, ah mean,
there's no pain no pressure no blood no nothin. Everythin's all
hazy.
Then it comes together bit by bit. Fuck me, it's offski. Offski-
pop, man. It's under there. Ma han. Under twenty ton of shit,
man. Aw, holy fuck ma han ma han ma han. The right one too.
Ma fuckin favourite. Ma auld writin wavin wankin han.
Fucked. Fucked for ever.

SCREAM.

Ah'm screamin an kickin an tearin the auld tonsils out but it
makes no odds, man. Naw, ah'm just fartin against thunder cos
the auld gulley motor's howlin like a hippo with a headache
an Denzo can't hear a thing. Not that the cunt's interested
anyway cos it's so dreich an dreary an every fucker's depressed.
That's what this town does to people, it grinds them down, so
it does, grinds them down.

Look ye can see it, see it on their faces. Everywhere ye look,
sad an lonely people with sad an lonely faces everywhere ye
fuckin look.
So sad.
Every cunt's so sad an lonely.

Just so happens a sad wee person's walkin by.
This sad wee wummin with a sad wee wean in a sad wee
go-chair sees yours truly lyin flat out.
Bambi on ice. Another failed attempt.

Denzo clocks the look on her her face, the look that says,
SHOCK HORROR
the works, painted on her boat race. Pointin. She's pointin
down here an screamin at this big black rubber lump gobblin
up ma arm.

Denzo flips his lid. Aw naw. Aw naw.
Ah mean, he felt the bump, felt the wheel bumpin over
somethin but he didn't know, did he? Naw, he thought it was
a boulder or a bottle or a big lump of ice or somethin. How
the fuck was he to know?
He fears the worst doesn't he? Aye, he fears the worst cos his
name is Denzo. Denzo fuckin Doom. He starts imaginin it's
ma head.
Aw, Jesus Christ Almighty, man.
He can see it now, so he can. A fuckin burst head trapped under
the wheel, burst like a baboon's arse an its tongue's hangin
out an it's got these big mental bloodshot eyes starin out it
like the darkest depths of hell an it's gonni haunt him forever,
man, it's gonni haunt his tortured soul. All he can think of
is blood.

Blood blood blood blood blood. Gallons of blood pishin out
onto the street. The gulley motor floatin in it.

He reverses back.
Aw, holy fuck, can't bear to look. No cunt can. No cunt. Me,
Denzo, the wee sad wummin with the wee sad wean. We just
can't bear to look, man. Can't.

Ah prise the peepers open slow, so ah do. Aye, nice an slow.
Aw lumpin fuck, man. Look. All ah see is this arm holdin two
pound of mince.
Aye, two pound of raw mince comin out ma wrist an the smell

of a slaughterhouse waftin off the steamy blood tricklin down
ma arm.
Everythin's birlin round, the wummin, the wean, the gulley
motor, the sky. The whole fuckin lot's birlin round, gettin
faster an faster an goin hazy an grey an dark an darker an
black.

The next thing ah know everythin's white
pure white.
White sheets white ceilin white walls. A beautiful white angel
with a lovely smile. Aw, check those pearly whites.

What the fuck's that, man? A candy floss. Aye, a big fluffy
candy floss comin out ma wrist. Swearit, man that's what
it's like.
Ah'm banaged up NHS style.
NHS? Aw, in the name of Christ. It comes together slow.
Monklans General Hospital. Ah'm in the fuckin Monklans.
The wee nurse is givin me a wakey-wakey type shake.
What a beauty. Can't take ma eyes of her. Think ah've died an
gone to heaven. She's talkin. Talkin to me so sweet. Tellin me
there's somebody here, somebody to see me.
Aw, what a beauty, man. What a beauty.
Beauty an the Beast.
Just saw the beauty.   Now meet the beast.

Aye, there's the beast. The Mad Dog.
There he is standin at the bottom of the bed. Big gappy smile.
Smilin at yours truly. Aye, man, grinnin like the proudest cat
in Cheshire.

Ye done it ma man, ye fuckin done it, he goes. Ye meant it
didn't ye? Ah knew it. Fuckin well knew it. Talk about big
balls. Ah'll tell ye somethin, sir, you've got bigger balls than a

West African elephant, so ye have. Some pair of balls, buddy.

Check it out, man. Check it.

Mad Dog called me buddy.

Buddy.

That's how it started, man.

Me an Mad Dog.

Buddies.

Chapter Five.
The suave city slicker.

Buddies?
Aye, that will be shinin bright.
Mad Dog had no buddies when it came to cash.

Wait till ah tell ye this.

We're workin outside the Town Hall. The Crazy Gang. Aye, by now we're called the Crazy Gang.
Me, Mad Dog, Chuck Mcfuck an Crazy D.

We're pink lint, so we are. Fuckin stony broke. Well it's Monday, innit? See Mondays, man. Hate Mondays.
The Boomtown Rats, that's what they used to call us.
Aye, yees are the fuckin Boomtown Rats so yees are, yees don't like Mondays, do yees?
They dubbed D 'Daisy'. Aye, daisy comes to work an daisy doesn't.

So anyway, where was ah? Aye, we're outside the Town Hall an this dude in a suave suit straight out the catalogue struts up. He's smilin. Always smilin these cunts, so they are.

Mad Dog hates smilin happy cunts. Ye know the type ah'm on about. Smilin happy-heads. Loads to be happy about.
Big fuckin smart guy, shiny silver car. Pulls all the blonde birds. None left for me an you, right? Big blondes with big tits go for happy-heads. Some guys have all the luck, bro.
Who's a pretty boy then?
Mad Dog gets ready. Ready to start on him.
The big cunt's one of them. Works in the Town Hall, doesn't

he? He's one of them. An office wallah, a fuckin faceless
wonder that lives off the sweat an shit of the common man.
He cuts our throats, the bastart.
That's his job. Cut this cut that. It's all we ever hear, cutbacks
cutbacks cutbacks. All down to cunts like him. Fuckin cutback
men.
It's us against them. He's one of them. Them.

Mad Dog's psyched up. He's goin that shivery way. Ready to
go, give it the business, give the pretty boy the one-two one-
two. Aye, here ye are, bang bang bang bang. Fuck your
pretty little arse, pretty boy.
Mad Dog can't make his mind up whether to fuck him or fight
him.

Hold it. Hold on there. Don't jump the gun, big guy.
Mad Dog's a cunt for jumpin the gun.

He holds it. Takes a breath. Benefit of the doubt time. Give the
poor cunt a chance, man. Fuckin liberty.

The suit's posh so he is. Oh yes yes yes, ever so posh.
An he's just wondering if any of us chaps happened to have
lost money.

Check the Dog, man. What's he like? His big ears start glowin
like uranium.
Aw, for fuck sake, a whole different ball game now, innit?
Listen by the way, who the fuck moved those goalposts?
Own up, ya bastart.

Mad Dog's up like a vomit. He realises the suave guy's a good
yin. Big honest cunt.
Hard to believe, so it is. One of them being honest. Strange.
Still.

OK, let's get ready to rumble. Big picture time. Mad Dog Goes To Hollywood. Equity card.
Hey listen, Mad Dog's some actor. Honest to fuck. The big guy could put Tom Cruise on a three-day week. Just watch him.

Eh, wait an ah'll check, he says to the suit.

He starts pattin his arse n stickin his hans in his hippers. Let me see now, he goes, batterin his chest like a gorilla.

He checks the shirt pockets.
Whistle whistle whistle.
His big mad eyes flash round the gang sendin out secret messages.
His eyeballs say it all.
They say, Start lookin too, ya cunts. Start rummagin. C'mon, for fuck sake, there's a move on here. A gift horse.
Fuckin found money. Go for it. Go go go go go!

What are we like? All tarry-arsed an sticky. Riflin through the pockets. Faces serious, all clockin each other.

Problem. Serious problem.

How much? How much has he found? We dunno do we?
Ah mean, if we dunno that, well, fuck.

We're hopin he's gonni say somethin. The suit.
Aye, we're hopin he'll bail us out seen as we're all strugglin.
Aye, that would be nice.

But naw. Naw, nothin. Not a cheep. Just stans there smilin.
Watchin us pawin away at the pockets lookin more an more confused. We're runnin out of pockets, man. We've fuckin checked everywhere. Down our socks, down our keks, up our arses, under our foreskins. You name it, we've fuckin checked it.

Runnin out of options.

Guess? Aye, take a guess.

But ye can't, man, ye can't, it's too risky. Ye've got too many choices, that's the fuckin problem.
Fiver? Tenner? Twenty? Could be any fuckin thing.
Naw, can't chance it. Ah mean, if yer wrong it's gone, man.
Gone for ever an the big dude offski. Offski-pop. Aye.
Aw, just imagine it, fuck. Imagine the suit goin, Oh ever so sorry chaps, I'll just pop down an han it in at the local Bobbies.

Ask him? Aye, fuck it, just ask the cunt. Go for it. Go for broke. Nothin to lose, have ye? Naw.
Mad Dog asks him, asks him how much he's found.

But this guy hasn't got where he is today bein a thicko, did he? Naw. Computers. He does computers, right? Money money money. That's his game, innit? Figures. Don't talk to the suit dude about figures. Fuck sake, the big guy can make them talk. Make them sing an dance.
Ye see, this is it. This is the thing. The difference. The big guy's got it up top. Knows all the dodges. Aye. Got the fuckin edge.

He gives us the look. Y'know the one. Squinty smile an sneerin eyes that say, C'mon now chaps, if you've lost money surely to blazes you know how much.

Time's runnin out. The suit's shruggin. He's ready to do a runner.

Bastart. Fuckin bastart, man. Down to the Bobby Shop his arse. Right into the big cunt's hipper it's goin. Fuckin cert.

Ye can picture it.
Aye, ah see it now. It's beamed live across ma mindscreen.

The hippest bar in Trendyville. The suave guy bummin off his load.

Oh gosh, I mean, really, it was an absolute scream. Honest to goodness. The look on the big hairy one's face when I asked him how much he had lost.

Ye can just picture it so ye can. All these eggheads an west end girls rollin about the place pissin their silk panties.

No chance. Can't let it happen. No way. Got to do somethin. Do somethin quick for fuck sake. Think think think.

Don't panic, man, stay calm. Have a smoke. Aye, there's an idea. Lum up.

Here big yin, have a smoke.

Mad Dog's still got the head buried in the wallet. Still rummagin like fuck givin it loads of the auld, Eh, eh, eh, let me check now, let me check.

Ah ask the suit for a light. Gimmee a light big yin, ah say.

Aw, check the lighter. A gold Ronson. He flicks it an out flashes this rich yellow flame burnin like the sun.

It hisses like a serpent as it hits ma soggy dog-end.

Check the big suave guy. Aw, check the boat race. What a picture. He's leanin back lookin at the sky. His head's up his arse. Can't get away from me fast enough.

His face says it all. Fuckin riff-raff. Scum. He's had enough, so he has.

Ah mean, ma tarry skin's touchin his. Aye. Fuck him.

Ah wrap my two hans round his an squeeze as ah get a light. Aye, just a wee light squeeze. But that wee light squeeze was all it took. All it took, man. An ah'll tell ye how.

Cos that's when ah spied it. Aye, look, man. Look. I spy with

my little eye somethin beginnin with P... purple.
A pinky purple.
There it was. Keekin out through his fingers like a ruby red
rose openin its petals on a bright summer morn.
Honest to fuck by the way, that's what it was like, man.
A hard hot knob-end oozin out yer foreskin.

Yessssssssss.

Easy does it now. Easy. Stay cool. Take deep breaths an blow in
an out slow.
Ah take two side-steps. Ah'm over his shoulder. Ah look down
the barrels of the Mad Dog's eyes.
Ah let the auld lips roll round the letters

T W E N T Y.

Mad Dog's knees are jelly. His head's lighter than a hobo's
hold-all. Back out with the Equity card.

Let me see now, he goes, studyin his wallet.
Ten quid for fag money, couple ah pound for bus-fare, thirty
notes for poll tax, couple ah quid for papers. Aw, ya bastart.
Twenty. Ah've dropped twenty.

Suave's got mixed emotions. What could've been, eh?
A couple of free Vodka-tinis down Trendyville havin a giggle
with the chicks. Still, never mind. One good deed an all that
shit. His wrist twists like magic.
Hey presto. There it is, man. Shiny new note. Sharper then the
crease down his breeks.
Mad Dog's paw zaps it like a lizard's tongue

ziiiiiiiiiiiiiiiiiiiiiiiiiiiiiiiiiiiiiiiiiiiiiiiiiipp

a hazy blur. Invisible to the naked eye.

Ah'm tellin ye by the way, Sugar Ray wouldn't've dodged it.
Its crispness crunches like a late November leaf.
All in one swift swoop it's halved, halved again, an into the
wallet. Snap. Shut. Into the hipper. Safe an sound, man.
Outa sight outa mind. Happy daze.

Now the gran finale. Mad Dog becomes a happy-head.
Can't thank the guy enough.
Ye're a star, he goes. Honest to fuck, man, a life-saver. Dunno
what ah'd've done all week. Wife an four weans too.

He's not finished there but. Naw.
Hanshakes all round.
C'mon now troops shake the man's han. Helluva nice of him.
Not many honest guys left, eh?
Mad Dog hugs him. Bear hug.

Fuck, look at big suave guy now, man. Died an gone to Hell.
Oh Holy Mother of God. The big guy. His face is a nippy mint.
Oh my God oh my God. What if somebody sees him.
Imagine it. Trendyville tonight. Eggheads goin, Oh Roger,
guess who we saw today hugging an kissing riff-raff.
Suave's finished. Street cred's dead.
An now he stinks. Stinks like an auld fuckin boiler house. An
check his suit. Fucked. The good suit's a goner. Finished. Gonni
burn it when he gets home.
Mad Dog tells him that's a pint he owes him. Tells him to call
down the boozer at lousin time. Aye, big yin, he says. Call
down the Argyll Bar, man, couple ah beers, couple ah swift
halfs, eh?

The poor cunt fucks off sharpish. Disappears quicker than a
knob-end at an orgy.
We all look at each other an then let out a big almighty

YEEEEEEHHHAAAAAAAAAAAAAAAAAAAAAHHHHHHHHHHH.

We're givin it high fives low fives back flips front flips
summersaults double solkos triple solkos five spins in the air
with a neat twist before landin. You name it, man we're doin
it, the Crazy Gang are doin it, so they are.
Ah'm tellin ye by the way, we're the fuckin synchronised
jumpin up in the air Olympic champions.

So once it all settled down ah turned to Mad Dog an went,
Right big man, didn't ah do well or what, eh, eh? Did ah not
play a stormer or did ah not play a stormer? Must be on to
halfers, eh?

D'ye know what he done? D'ye know what the big bastart
went an done? He turned the fuckin palms out an put on that
innocent-as-an-altar-boy face an went, Aw, honest to fuck ma
man, ah did drop a twenty. Swear on ma weans's life ah did.

That's what the bastart went an done, man.
Fly as a bag ah weasels.

Still, there wasn't a great deal ah could do about it, was there?
Naw.
Ah just went away an sat in the hut an cursed the big cunt
upside down under ma breath.
Aye, man, under ma breath.

Chapter Six.
Fuck em all bar Nancy.

Greenvalley. Oooh yes how lovely. Lovely jubbly.

Greenvalley.

Green. Lots of green.
The green green grass of home.
Acres upon acres of rollin hills an flushin meadows. Auld granny cottages with wee thatched roofs tucked under the oxters of towerin oaks. Birds chirp an rivers trickle. The smell of fresh hay.

Greenvalley!

Picture-postcard stuff. The Cotswolds eat yer heart out, right? Wrong.
Wine alleys an shootin galleries an shitey-arsed weans with snotty noses.
Four-in-a-block houses with the matchin plywood curtains an metal doors. The houses have just been painted too. Aye, check the lovely paintwork.

NOBBER   SKIN

YOUNG PIRATES ROOL YA BASS

JANICE SUCKS DiCKS

FAT DANNY TAKES IT UP THE ARSE

Aye, all done in screamin bright colours.
Ye want to see the streets too. Honest to fuck, the streets would put Riley's scrap-yard out the game.

Rusted car carcasses outside every door.
Got to watch the auld lorry down here, ah'm tellin ye.
They'll have it up on bricks in two ticks.
Tyres? Fuck me, man, they're mad for them. It's a fact. If
they're round an made of rubber, they're offski. Quick as a
flash. No low-flyin aircraft round here bud, no way. Have the
fuckin wheels off a jumbo if it drops too low.

An ye want to see the weans. Aw the weans, man, look at the
poor weans. Skinny tight-eyed weans in tartan shirts an
dungarees. Banjo boys. Mad Dog calls them banjo boys.
Ye know the kind ah'm talkin about, man.
Mah big brother's mah Daddy.

Deliverance. Ever see the film *Deliverance*?
Mad Dog's favourite. Saw it thirty-eight times. Ye want to hear
him doin all the voices. Shit hot, so he is. He puts on the auld
southern drawl.

Hey lil kiddy, where you learn ta play banjo like that?
Ah'll be dawg gone.

An ah'll tell ye what else. The place is full of hing-outs.
The hing-outs are hingin out the windows. Watch the fuckin
hing-outs, man.
See the minute they see workmen, their pussies start poutin
like fuckin rose petals. Ye know what ah'm sayin? It's the auld
wage-packet thing. The minute they know ye lift a wage-
packet yer a meal ticket for her an the nine weans.

How's about it, big boy? Come up an see me some time.
Ooooh ah'm all yours.

Ah'm tellin ye, by the way. Watch yerself. The sluts are up to
all sorts. Mad Dog didn't care but. Didn't give a fuck.

Ye know that sayin, fuck em all bar Nancy?
Not Mad Dog. Mad Dog fucks em all. Fucks em all bar nobody.
Nobody. No exceptions, no rules, no lines ye don't cross, no
levels ye don't stoop below. None. Ah'm tellin ye, every
fucker's fair game.

Mad Dog. Aye. A true dog, man. A real reservoir dog on heat.

He ended up fuckin this burd called Nancy. Every day he'd
disappear up the stairs to her house. Aye, he'd just turn round
an go, Right lads, ah'm offski.

Offski-pop he'd go, doin the Mad Dog walk. Head back, chest
out, fists clenched, big cheesy grin. Edges of the mouth hittin
the ear-holes.
Off to fuck Nancy.
Know the worst thing about it, by the way? He's got to come
back out an tell ye all about it.
Well, that's half the fuckin fun, innit?

Honest lads, ah just got in the door an she whipped off ma
joggers. Ripped them right off my arse, man.
Gaggin for it, so she was.
Aye, an then she sunk the auld laughin gear right round ma
trumpet an very near sooked it raw. Heh listen to this, ah fired
it all over her boat race, man. The bold Nancy. Aye, dived on
top of ma doaber. Fuckin impaled herself on it, so she did.
Whit a bit ah ridin we done, lads, honest. Bangin away all day.
Five-ten-double-ten-double-ten-a-hundred.

Mad Dog an Nancy bare-arse boxin. Just the tarry boots on
too. Aye, Mad Dog keeps the boots on.

Fuck aye, man, it's a must, he'd go. Ah mean, ye never know,
do ye? Can't be too careful. Ye've heard all the stories about

guys givin it the auld five-ten-double-ten, an all along there's
some wide fucker hidin in the wardrobe watchin. Aye,
watchin, waitin, waitin his chance. Next thing ye know, bang,
he's dancin all over yer back givin ye a right good bleechin an
takin all yer cash. Ah mean, it's hard goin tryin to scrap when
yer starkers an all gooey balled an nothin on the feet, man. If
ye're in yer bare feet ye've no chance. Fuck that.

The Mad Dog keeps the boots on.
Fucks em all, man. Mad Dog fucks em all.

Don't give us yer pish, he'd say. Don't give me none of this
wouldn't-ride-Nancy-with-yours crap. Don't give me that shit,
man. Don't give me it.
Ah mean, yer lyin there full of the wine an ye look down an
there she is, the bold Nancy blowin blue murder out yer
trumpet sendin fifty-volt shock waves roarin up yer arse.
What ye gonni do, eh? What the fuck ye gonni do?
Tell her to fuck off?
Now now, Nancy, stop that, stop that right now, stop it.
Aye, that will be shinin bright.
Don't give me any yer shit. When yer drunk enough yer knob
rules, OK.

It was down at Greenvalley the carry-on with wee Taw
happened. Aw, fuck, man wait till ye hear this. Listen, ah'm
tellin ye. Pure classic so it was.

There was this wee cunt called Taw, right?
Wee Taw. Banjo boy. An X-ray in a duffle coat.
Used to hang about the hut all day.
Aye, he hung on ye like a too-big coat, so he did. Never failed
to show up, either. The wee cunt would be up at the crack ah
dawn listenin for the truck trundlin up the road.

The minute we hit the street he'd be right over at us gibberin
like a senile budgie.
Ye want to have heard him. GBH to the lugs.

Alright, troops, howzit goin? Any rammies? Any smokes?
Gies a fag big guy, go'n, please. Lookin for any helpers, eh?
Ah can shovel, ah can rake, ah can drive a lorry, no probs.
Give's a shot of yer lorry. Need any gear, troops? Ah'm yer
man, the Taw boy here's yer man. Have ye got a motor big guy,
have ye? Needin a wireless? Ah've got a wireless, a fuckin
beauty, still in the box, by the way, an absolute belter. Ni-cam
twin speakers, stereo sounds, double tape deck, the works, man,
the fuckin works, straight up. Aye, just give's the nod big yin.
Ah'm yer, man.

Well, normally Mad Dog can't be arsed with weans.
He normally goes, Weans? Fuckin weans? Hunt them to fuck.
Bigger pests than the Colorado Beetle.
So we were waitin on it. Waitin on him huntin the wee filla to
fuck, givin it the auld if-ye-don't-get-to-fuck-ye'll-get-the-auld-
size-ten-right-up-the-arse warnin. But it was a shocker what
happened next. A real shockarooney shot.
Wait an ah'll tell ye what happened.

Mad Dog turns round an lobs the Taw a snout.
Aye, honest to fuck by the way. An listen to this.
He starts givin the wee man a lecture. Couldn't believe it.
Couldn't.

Listen wee man, he goes, Ye shouldn't be smokin, ah'm tellin
ye, it stunts yer growth. Aye, n listen to what ah'm sayin, see
the fags, slow ye down so they do, dry up the auld engine,
drain the power. Listen son, see if ye've no power or speed,
ye've fuckin had it. Goosed, shafted, up muggers' lane with no

chib, right? See what ah'm sayin? Ye got it?

Taw starts bobbin an weavin. Up on his toes, throwin light jabs.
Oooof ooooof oooof. Ah can fight, big guy, he's yelpin.
Ah've got speed, ah've got speed, oooof oooof oooof, plenty juice in the Taw boy's engine. Plenty.

Mad Dog's wearin a strange look. A look ye don't see on him too often, man. A poor-wee-cunt's-not-got-much-goin-for-him-an-reminds-me-of-me-when-ah-was-a-boy sort of look. Aye. Strange.

Next thing ye know, he goes like that an throws the wee guy a deuce.
Here wee guy, he says, here's a couple of quid. Go'n home. Go'n.

So anyway, this was goin on for a while. Wee Taw comin up to the hut yappin away a lot of shite an annoyin the fuckin heart out of every cunt. But Mad Dog kept havin hundreds of time for him. Kept lobbin him snout givin him money an teachin him how to box an all that.
Strange but. Still. No cunt bothered.

An then it happened.

Wee Taw just came right out with it.
Aye, he just turned round to Mad Dog one day an went

HEY BIG GUY, CAN YOU BE MA UNCLE?

Aw, honest to fuck by the way. Till the day ah die, swear to God ah'll never forget it. Never.
Time stopped. Yer breathin stopped. The whole fuckin world an its auntie stopped.

The words rang out forever an just hung in the air like a hot curried fart.
There was nowhere to look. Nothin to say. The auld brainbox just went on strike an refused point-blank to return to work.
Fuck ye, man. Can't think, can't think.
What do ye do, eh?

Ye know what it's like when that happens.
Ye feel little ripples of laughter ticklin yer inner skin an slitherin their way from yer toes right up into yer belly leavin this big laughter lump buildin up in yer throat.
An then the auld face muscles start twitchin don't they? Aye.
But ye don't dare laugh, man. Don't even think about it.
Laugh an yer fuckin dead. Dead.

Ye try to look away, right?
Where but? Where?

Ye look at Big Chuck an Crazy D. Aw, check the cunts out, man.
They're pullin more faces than Phil Cool.
Every fucker's wearin plastic faces.
Waitin. Waitin on somethin happenin.

Taw boy standin there gallus as fuck. No fear.

Can ye big guy? Can ye? Can ye? Eh? eh?

We're gonni bust. Me Crazy D an Chuck, man. Three plastic purple faces. Three Ribena men. Our bottom lips are wrapped round our necks.
We're waitin on it. Any second now we're expectin to see Mad Dog givin it, Ya cheeky little bastart, ah'll fuckin uncle ye.
An then ye expect to see the Taw filla flyin through the air with a metal toe-cap embedded in his sphincter.
That's what we were waitin for. Aye.

But hey, listen, ah'll tell ye this. We're still waitin. Ah'll tell ye how. It didn't fuckin happen, that's how.

Naw, did it fuck.

The Mad Dog just went like that an ruffled Taw's hair an dropped a just-clownin-about punch on his jaw.

By the way, Mad Dog's got all these different names for his punches.

A just-clownin-about punch is when the hairs on his knuckles just skiff the skin an no more.

Wee man, he goes. Wee man.

Fuck me. Strange, eh?

Aye, well, wait till ye hear the rest of it.

We're all down at Nancy's house this night. Nancy's den.
The Crazy Gang's gang bang den.

Ye want to see this.
As soon as ye walk in, the fuckin smell of dampness stale booze piss an mucky farts stabs you right up the hooter an stings yer eyes like acid. Gaggin.

Nancy's on the moon. A stalactite slabber hangin from the fangs. Greasy worms sproutin out her scalp. Quo's Down the Dustpipe crackles an jumps. Aye, even the fuckin record player's got the hump.

Jeez, man how'd ah get here? It's the drink. It's the fuckin auld swally, it sways ye. Just like Mad Dog says, when yer full of the auld swally yer champer rules.

Anyway, we all end up bare-arsed an heavy-bollocked

wearin nothin but tarry boots.

Yeeeeeeeeeeeee hah.
Gang bang gang bang.

Five-man gang bang. Five card trick.
Five baldy one-eyed serpents beefin Nancy.
One up the poo-nanny, one in the jacksie. One in each han
an one down the throat. Go baby go.
Nancy loves a whiskey lollipop.
Mad Dog dooks his doaber into his whiskey glass swirlin it
round stingin the nip's eye. He rams it right down Nancy's
throat an does the porn star voice.

Yeah baybee yeah. Aw, suck my cack. Aw, baybee baybee,
you suck my big thick cack so goooood.

Nancy's onto it like a starved mongrel.
Munch munch chomp.
Mad Dog's tongue's hangin down past his belly an he's gone
all slitty-eyed. Looks just like a little Greenvalley boy. Hey little
kiddy, play that Goddamn banjo.

Nancy throws her head back sendin a mane of slippery eels
slitherin down her back.
Next thing she starts goin,

Yeeeuuch uurrrrghhh yuuuuccckk.

She starts givin real heavy-duty boak. Aw, yuck, she goes.
There's fuckin lemonade in that.

Mad Dog raises a glass to the Devil an lets rip a hearty

HAAAARGHH HAAAAAAAARRGGGHH.

Jeez, man, this ain't happenin. Can't be. No way.

Ah'm shaggin manky Nancy. Bangin her, boys' gate style.
Pumpin like a fuckin oil rig.
It's the voddy, man. Too much voddy for the body.
Ma whole body's numb, ah'm tellin ye. Numb as a castrated
bollock. It's like beefin a blob of raw liver. Can't feel a thing,
man. Dunno if the auld pecker's hard, soft, in her jacksie or her
poo-nanny.
Dunno. Don't care.

Heebi jeebies, man. Aw, it's the fuckin heebies. It must be.
Nancy's arse is in the air. She's just a bag of bones. Lyin like a
carcass of a gobbled-up animal.

Snakes.

Aye, big fuckin yellow-eyed red-tongued snakes start oozin
out her rib-cage, slitherin like exotic belly dancers across the
greasy floor. Foamy fungus round the rim of her arse is movin,
man. It's blisterin an poppin. Big fuckin foosty maggots are
bungee jumpin from her pubes. Match-head-sized blood
bubbles pop out her pores an burst an sizzle, smellin of burnin
rat shit.
Holy Mother of Christ, man.
Reality? Nightmare?
It's fuckin heebi jeebi time. Aye, the auld heebi jeebi man's
in charge.
OK, brother. Welcome to hell.
Escape?
Yes.

The auld head-piece starts goin lighter than a porn star's baw
bag an the grey mist growls down on me like death. The eyes
go heavy.
The blackout's deep.

Two hundred thousan years later ah start to come round.
Aw, holy fuck, man. Where am ah? Where am ah where where
where?

Haunted house. Haunted. Words, words come back to haunt
me, man.
Mad Dog's do-anythin-when-yer-drunk words blare like an air-
raid siren blowin the stoor off ma brain.

Aw, Jesus Christ Almighty. Fucked. Ah've went an fucked
Nancy. Fucked her in the jacksie, so ah did.
Aye, her fuckin foosty fungus-ridden snake-infested jacksie.
Awww my God. Awwww. Right in front of every cunt too. Aw
my Christ. Ah'm finished, man. Well an truly finished. No way
back. Welcome to the Crazy Gang.
Ah'm all cold an shivery with a roughcast throat. Ah've got
tacky muck on ma tongue an gungy lips. Ah tear ma sticky
eyelids open slow an all ah see is

TAW.

Taw. Wee Taw, man. Ah'm face to face with Taw.
Aye, the little tartan-shirted Taw. Play that fuckin banjo boy.
Hey there boy, play me a little tune.

What are YOU doin here? ah say.

Naw, he says. What the fuck are YOU doin here? Where's ma
Maw?
His Maw? Nancy? Aw, holy lumpin fuck.

Mad Dog!!!   Nancy!!!   Taw!!!

Oh ya bastart. Got it now, man. Clear as a fresh-water
fountain. Aye, big Uncle Mad Dog. Fly big bastart.

Chapter Seven.
Big Chuck Mcfuck an the magic pies.

Fuckin burds, man. Burds.

Tarmen have bad luck with burds.

Ah remember one of the times Mad Dog's wife had ran away an left him. Aye, she used to leave him all the time so she did. Big Chuck Mcfuck had no such luck. His missus fucked him out.

Out, she told him. Out ya big drunken bastart. Who needs ye?

Out. No luck Chuck. No luck.

Mad Dog put the big man up. Aye, he gave him a room. Roof over yer head big man.

Heart of gold. Mad Dog had a heart of gold.

No bother Chucky boy, he says. Treat it like yer own. Just you an me, son, we'll show them. Show the bastarts.

Burds?

Ye know what they say.

Ye can't live with them. An ye can't live with them.

Mad Dog sent Chuck to Asda.

Told him, You do the shoppin an yer man'll do the cookin.

We'll do week about, eh? Week about.

Mad Dog tells him to get anythin he likes as long as he gets seven dinners. Doesn't matter what it is, man, doesn't matter a fuck cos Mad Dog can eat shite. Aye, eat anything at all. Scabby-arsed horses all round, man, it doesn't matter. As long as they're scrannin up every day, that's the main thing.

Aye, big yin get seven dinners. Got to feed the boat race, right?

Big Chuck Mcfuck but. Hey listen, the big man's not the brightest. Not the fuckin sharpest tool in the shed. Know what ah'm sayin?

Back he comes. Back he comes from Asda. Sure as fuck, seven bags of tatties seven tin of peas an seven chickens. Straight up, man. That's what he done.

Aye, Big Chuck was Mad Dog's lodger.
They were doin alright too. Aye, alright for a while. But then it started causin problems.
Big fuckin elephant's-dick-sized problems.
Wait till ah tell ye this.

They were out boozin this night an Mad Dog's up at the bar tryin to get the knickers off Big Stella the barmaid.

What are they like?
The Horny Dog an the Bitch on heat.
Big Stella's gaggin for it.
She's got FUCKME FUCKME FUCKME BABY all over her face.
Mad Dog's droolin at the mouth, man.
Stella's givin it heavy tease.
She's wipin the bar. Aye, wipin up the slabbers. A good hard wipe she's givin it, makin her big jugs judder like jellies an leanin right over showin off the cleavage. Check it out, man check out the cleavage. Listen, we're talkin trucker's arse here, ah'm tellin ye, fuckin trucker's arse.

She's out liftin the tumblers. Squeezin past Mad Dog rubbin the titties along his back. Just touchin an no more. Aye, the very tip of the nipple just gently skiffin the hairs on his back. Oh fuck aye, Big Stella knows what to do. Knows the ropes.

Mad Dog starts show-boatin. Ye know the style. Sleeves up,

chest out, fag between the lips. Big boy's burnin up, man. On fire. It's fuckin Nat King Cole time an he knows it. Mad Dog can smell it.

He bursts into his favourite chat-up line. Ye know the one. Three guys jumped him under the bridge at the canal. He lays it off to Stella.

Aw, for fuck sake what's he like, man?
Takin her through it blow by blow. She's lovin it too. Lovin it. Look at her. Awestruck. Leanin on the bar starin down his big mad eyes.
No words needed. Just actions. Watch all the actions.
The big chunky finger's pointin, tellin the cunts they're gettin it. See yous bastarts. Yous're gettin it.
Starts shadow boxin. Bobbin an weavin. Right up there at the bar, right in front of every cunt. Ah'm tellin ye, man, Mad Dog don't give a fuck. Bang bang bang bang, he goes, sprayin slabbers everywhere, throwin in the body shots the hooks the rights the lefts the uppercuts. Bang bang bang.
Then he holds his han up, palm open, tilts it over slow.
That's him showin ye how the guy went down, foldin like a tuppenny book.

CRASH

he rams the sole of his boot down on the kid-on head on the floor. Pointin at it, givin it a lecture. An then he swings a couple of boots at this other fucker with his head jammed in the railins.

Aye, down on his knees the cunt was with his head wedged tight screemin for mercy. Die ya bastart.

Then he starts pointin, man, pointin away down there at that other cunt, ye know, the third one. The one that done the runner. He's pointin after him. Ah'll get ye, ya fucker. Ah'll get ye. Aye, ye can fuckin run but ye can't hide.

The Dog stans up straight brushin hisself down then shrugs an turns the palms out.

Easy peezy, he tells her. Pure doddle.

Listen, Big Stella's impressed. Oh fuck aye.
Check out the big starin eyes with the pin-head pupils. Hot flushes an nipples peekin out like Tom Thumb cigars. The body lingo's screamin out blue murder CLIMB INSIDE THESE PANTIES BIG BOY. NOW.
Big Stella's ready. Ripe an ready.

Mad Dog lays it on the line, man, tells her straight.
Listen Doll, he goes, Ah'm not one for puttin too fine a point on it but this big hungry chomper here hasn't felt a bit of moist warmth in yonks.

He tells her he'd love to take her back home, turn her inside out, upside down n back to front. Ram it down her throat up her honey pot then squeeze it real tight right up her boys' gate.

Ooooooooooooooooooooh, Stella coos. The auld eyelids are flutterin, givin it a tiny blush-blush.

Thought ye'd never ask, she says. Thought ye'd never ask.

Mad Dog warns Big Chuck, Go for a walk. Get some scran. Go do some sight-seein. Sit in the public park an flash yer cock at the queers. Anythin ye like, man, just stay out the road, stay away, don't come home till ah'm done, man. Don't come back for at least three, four hours.

Mad Dog likes to take his time. Mad Dog's a stayer. Goes the distance all the time, man. All the time. All night long.

Big Chuck's been warned. Well warned.

Big Chuck boy's Hank Marvin. Says he could eat the scabs off a camel's cock.
Says he knows this great wee chippy. Best in the business, man. Does these fuckin big juicy steak pies. The best in the world, man, best in the world, aw, they're the berries, so they are, honest to fuck, man, can taste them right now so ah can.

Chucky boy's rantin an ravin away doin every fucker's head in.

Aw, these steak pies lads. Ye want to see the size of them. Chunks of meat the size of yer fist an the hot juicy gravy just flowin out them. Honest to fuck, lads, they are absolutely massive. Massive. Desperate Dan would have a fight on his hans, ah'm telling ye, a fifteen-rounder. An talk about tender? Fuck, they just melt, melt in yer mouth so they do.
Aye, the best steak pies in the town, best in the country, best in the planet, best in the universe.

Big Chucky's off an runnin, he's off an runnin. Thank fuck.
Just one thing on his mind.
Aye. A steak pie supper.

Mad Dog n Stella head back to the house. Both rampant. Both ready to rumble. Ten rounds of bare-arse boxin.
The door shuts behind them.
Bang, they go for it. Head-on collision. Chewin at faces, tongues down throats, hans clawin tits, balls, fanny, arses. Tearin off the clobber. Joggers n keks round knees n ankles n tryin to run upstairs. Not easy, man. Try it.
Mad Dog sinks the molars into her pap. She throws her head

back, hissin. She digs her claws into his big fuckin gorilla back
an starts draggin them down slow. Slow, man. Draggin them
down slow into his arse. Two big meaty cheeks. She draws a
han back n gives them a mighty skelp.
She digs in deeper breakin the skin. Tiny blood droplets trickle.
The Dog lets out a yelp n bites into her shoulder mufflin the
sound, stiflin the pain.

Aw, the pain, man the pain.
Mad Dog's wincin. Eyes waterin. Arse like a fuckin pin-cushion.
Real heavy-duty arse pain.

Come on now, who's a big babby, Stella goes, pullin his head
into her hot an meaty mounds. Aw, big baby, come to
Mamma, come to Mamma.

They crash onto the bed. Hot sweaty bodies bang together.
Dull farty noises rumblin like thunder. Arses buckin, hips
thrustin, givin it dry ride.
Let's get rhythm baby. Let's get rhythm.
They birl round like Come Dancing. 69. Stella munchin his
chomper.
Mad Dog's muffin the mule. Slurp slurp slurp.
Givin it the finger. Two. Three. Four. In past the knuckles, past
the wrist.
Stella's pussy's suckin like a gulley motor drawin shite out a
drain. Aw, what a pussy, man. Hot an gooey pussy. Pussy like a
bill-poster's pail. Can't throw a length up there, man. No
chance. Drag out yer bollocks by the roots.
Buns to an elephant.
No way José. Not goin in there.

Mad Dog birls her round. Arse in the air. Little star-shaped
arsehole, tight as two coats of paint an throbbin like a frog's

throat. Aw, yes, man, yes yes yes yes. There it is, smilin up at him like a bloomin red rose, its poutin ruby lips blowin him kisses. Mad Dog can't believe it. What's it like? Like a burnin hot coal glowin in the dark. Oh fuck aye, man. Red hot arsehole.
That's where it's goin, man. His big beef dagger. Right up there boy. Right up there.

Next thing ye know there's this big fuckin almighty crash.
Aye, big Chucky boy comes crashin through the door holdin his belly an doubled up in pain as if he's been plunged.
He crumples up on the bed lettin rip with these whiney moans.
Aw, aw, aw, aw, awwww ma belly ma belly. Says somethin inside him's died. It's died, man. It's turnin fuckin toxic an eatin his insides. Says it feels like a steak knife bein thrust in him.

Awww awwww aw, the pain, can't stan the pain.

He curls up like a cobra an starts gouchin. Short sharp jerks.
Legs shakin, feet kickin out in spasms. His back arches an a pair of trainers shoot through the air.
Whooosh, there he goes, man, a pole-vaulter catapultin across the room.

He whips down the joggers in mid-stride. Like ah said before, man, runnin with the auld keks round yer knees ain't easy.
Runnin with the keks round yer knees an skittery shite oozin through yer fingers is harder still.
The big man makes for the lavvy. A mad frantic dash.
Dull gurgly sqwelchy noises rattle through the air. Has he made it? Dunno.
Mad Dog doesn't know. Doesn't care. The party's over. The muscle tissue softens on his ramrod. Gettin softer an softer, goin floppy.

He slaps it off her arse. Nothin. He talks to it. Aye, Mad Dog
talks to his dick, honest. Come on big filla he goes, don't let
me down, stan tall for the big man.
Na, nothing. It just hangs its head in shame. The little withered
winky with the shrivelled pink face stares at the floor. What's it
like, eh? Scolded schoolboy.

An the fire goes out in Stella's arsehole. Big moist pussy no
more, man. Big slabbery lips curlin up like an autumn leaf,
goin dry an crispy.
Home time. On with the gear. Big Stella's offski. Offski-pop.

Bye-bye big boy, she says to Mad Dog on the way out. What a
pity, eh? What a night it could've been. What we could've
done. Could've beefed me deep an hard all night. All night
long. Deep an hard.
Oh yes big boy, just picture it. Me, hot n tight, slidin up n
down on yer shaft an grindin on yer bollocks crackin them like
conkers an birlin round sittin on yer face an eatin up yer loins.
Aw, yes yes yes, big boy, what a night it could've been.
Ach well, not to worry, she says. Mibbee some other time.
Then again mibbee not.

Ever seen a grown man cry?
Mad Dog lies there like Christ on the cross. Gutted. Can't
believe it, man. Can't be happenin. No way. One second yer on
a fluffy warm cloud floatin towards the edge of Heaven. Then
thud. Yer arse hits the cold pissy floors of Hell.
Lyin there shell-shocked. Cold an soggy loins.
He's gonni kill Big Chuck, man. Gonni crack his head. Bastart's
gonni die for this one.

Not tonight though. Na, no point. Can't catch him. Tomorrow.
Kick his cunt in tomorrow.

Like ah say, man, no chance of catchin Chuck. No chance. Big cunt's whizzin through the room like a wasp with a hard-on. In an out the bog all night, man. Back an forward back an forward. Talk about shitin. Listen, this is fuckin eye of a needle stuff. Sanblastin the enamel of the cludgy. Aw, the name-ah-fuck, man.

Know what it sounded like?

The gulley motor. Honest to fuck by the way. Sounded like the gulley motor drawin ten ton of shit out a stank. Swear it. Either that or Big Stella's pussy. Take yer pick.

Aw, the poor big cunt's arse, man, ah'm tellin ye, it would put a farmer's shit-spreader out the game, no bother.

Hey, an not only that, ye want to have seen the fuckin mess. Aw, in the name ah fuck, man, it was everywhere. Shite n fuckin spew all over the walls, carpets, curtains, sink. You name it.

An right there in the middle of it all's Big Chuck Mcfuck stuck with his arse down the pan an his head in the sink, pukin. Pukin an shittin away with the smell waftin up an burnin his eyes, burnin his arsehole. Aw, his poor arsehole's fuckin nippin. Nippin like napalm. Glowin so it was, aye, his big arse glowin like a hot coal in the dark. Just like big Stella's. The cunt had to watch Mad Dog didn't put the boot up it. Mad Dog's got a thing about arseholes. This arsehole's dead meat but. Dead meat. Tomorrow Mad Dog's gonni kill him. Tomorrow.

Next day they head out to work. Mad Dog doesn't speak. Never does in the mornin. Na, Mad Dog's not a much of a mornin person.

Strange. Unpredictable. Can never tell what he's thinkin. Ye just don't know.

Check Big Chucky boy standin over there. What's he like?
Peely-wallied up. Colour of death.
Can't eat. No way, man. Can't eat, drink, smoke, pish, shite.
Nothin. Too sore. Everythin hurts. Hurts like fuck.
He just stans there wearin the auld puppy-pissed-the-carpet look.

Poor big cunt can't even sit down, so he can't. Naw, just stans there like a spare dildo in a whorehouse.

Mad Dog clocks him. Gives him the look. Ye know that one that burns right through ye? Aye, that one. He gives him that one then looks away.

The big guy's sphincter muscles are goin like that, bleet bleet bleet. His big burst strawberry arsehole's throbbin an he's vibratin like a ten-inch dildo. What the fuck's goin on, man, what's goin on?
Mad Dog's sayin nothin. He's just actin like nothin's happened, man. But he keeps givin him those looks.
Fuck me. Nightmare. Ah'm tellin ye, it's worse not knowin.

Aw, come on to fuck an get it over with, Big Chuck's thinkin. He would rather just get his kickin an be done with it. See all this waitin, it'd drive ye fuckin mad.

He tries some chit-chat, the usual pish, lickin Mad Dog's arse, tellin him how shit-hot at pool he was last night an askin him about Big Stella.
What about her, good ride, eh? Those tits, hey, ah'll tell ye ah wouldn't mind a sook at them myself, so ah wouldn't. An they fuckin thighs, an that arse. Fuck me, bet she knows what the

auld fanny's for, eh? Bet ye gave her a right good seein-to, big man. Bet ye did, eh?

He goes for broke. Fuck it. Pushes his luck. Says, Hope ah didn't put ye off like, ye know, eh, that wee bit of bother ah had last night, ye know, mibbee somethin ah had to eat like, eh, ye know how it is big guy, helluva sorry so ah am.

He gets another look. Aye. Another burns-right-through-ye look.
Mad Dog's that mad he looks at him like he's got a good mind to put him on the Stop n Go.

Aw, listen. Now there's a thing. The auld Stop n Go. Ah'm tellin ye, avoid it like a crabbed up pussy.

Ah'll tell ye all about that after.

Anyway, Mad Dog just lets him suffer. Lets him suffer all mornin.
Right up until dinner-time.
Dinner-time. Every fucker's Hank Marvin.
Mad Dog stares hard at Chuck. Big mad stare. Doesn't look away this time. Naw, just keeps starin. Points the big finger at him an rolls it back.

C'mere you ya cunt, he goes.

This is it, Chuck reckons. This is it. Kickin time. Ah well. Let's get it over.

But Mad Dog's calmed down by now, right. Decides to let Big Chuck off the hook. Strange, eh? Decides it's not his fault any more, reckons it's the cunt that sold him the pie's fault. The cunt that owns the chippy. The one that sells the MAGIC pies. Those fuckin best-in-the-world, best-he's-ever-tasted, lovely-juicy-tender-chunks-of-meat-the-size-of-bulls-balls STEAK N KIDNEY PIES.

It's all his fault. Aye, the chippy man. Bastart. All his fuckin fault, so it is.

Mad Dog reckons he's gonni teach the cunt a lesson. Teach him not to sell any more foosty fuckin pies. Won't ruin any other poor cunt's night, so he won't.

No way, man. The guy's gettin it.

Gonni knock him out, bang bang bang.
Gonni wreck his shop. Sold his last pie the fly bastart.

Mad Dog sticks his chest out an tells Chuck to lead the way.

Aye, you go first an we'll follow. Magic chippy, here we come.

Off we go, marchin through the main street, Big Chuck at the front with the shoulders drooped an the head bowed, snivellin away. Mad Dog's right at his back givin it heavy-duty swagger, man. Givin it gangster walk.

Big Chuck's lookin about as if he's lost. All confused to fuck, so he is. Standin there twiddlin the hairs on his chin an nibblin his fingers.

Can't remember where it was, he says. Can't. Fuckin can't mind, can't say for sure, aw fuck, ye know what it's like when yer full of that drink an the auld shutters roll down on the mind piece. Ah've had a blackout lads, honest. Ah mean, there's that, many chippies about an they all look alike. Know what ah mean?

OK, Mad Dog goes, Gave ye a wee chance didn't ah? Aye. Ah was gonni go easy on ye. Throw ye a wee lifeline. But if ye say ye can't remember, well, ah'm just gonni have to kick seven shades of shite out yer arse then.

There it's, over there!, says Chuck.

Luigi's Fish an Chicken Bar. Best in Town, says the sign in the window.
Oh aye, man, best in town. Best in the whole wide world, best in the planet, best in the universe, the fuckin best ever, man. Best ever. Mad Dog's knows all about it. Heard it all before, so he has. Had it up to here with all that shit. Fuckin Tally bastart. Mad Dog doesn't like the Tallies. Bunch of pricks, man. Pussies. He marches over. Marches in. Place is jumpin too. Every cunt turns an sees us all standin. Sees Mad Dog grindin the teeth an clenchin the fists.

Silence all round.   。

There's this wee podgy guy behind the counter with the greasy forehead three chins an four bellies.
His wee happy smile an warm eyes roll across the shop clockin Mad Dog.
The wee happy smile an warm eyes do a runner.
Sweat beads like rivet heads start poppin out his forehead. Wee greasy forehead. His eyes roll on to Chuck. Slight smile, slight sense of relief, then back to Mad Dog.

Big mad-eyed Dog. More sweat beads. Is the wee man tense or what? Listen, ye couldn't get a bus ticket between the wee man's arse cheeks. Honest to fuck by the way, ye couldn't prise his arse open with a pinch bar. Never saw anythin like it. ·
Give him his due but. He tries to bluff it. Tries to act like nothin's wrong. Gives it Tally twang.

Yes-a-lads, what-ah-d'ya-want?

This is not what Mad Dog expected. Naw. Not what he wanted. He wanted some big raven-haired suave guy with the swarthy good looks. Ye know the type? Fuckin drippin in gold an rings on all the fingers. Mad Dog was hopin he'd start givin him lip, start gettin gallus. Big man could just leap the counter an bang bang bang knock him out there an then. Aye, that's what he hoped for. Not this. Some poor cunt's granpappy. Some poor wee roly poly sweaty guy. Sixty odd.

See the thing with Mad Dog is, the big cunt can't take liberties. Wishes he could, sometimes. Aye. Ah mean, it would've made life a whole lot easier if he'd just battered big Chuck there an then an just been done with it. But naw. The big man just cannot take liberties. Can't. Just can't, man. Never could.

He lays it on the line to Luigi. He tells him about last night. Tells him straight. Says, Look wee man, last night yer man here was at the edge of Heaven. He turns an points at Chuck an says, Ah'm just about to polish ma knob an this big fucker here stoats in sayin some pie he's ate has turned foosty an that it's poisoned his stomach. Well doesn't he start spewin it out his arse all night, man. Firin it all over the fuckin place. Near gassin every cunt to death, so he was. Well, no burd in her right mind's gonni tolerate that, eh? No chance. The auld pussy just clams up like an arsehole in a gay gang rape. Goes as dry as the Gobi desert. So she's offski-pop. Up, clobber on, out the door, offski. Offski-pop, leavin yours truly lyin there twiddlin the auld bollocks.
So, not a very good night all round, eh? Not a story any fucker'd want to tell their granweans, is it?
So ye see, the pie's the problem. Aye, that's the problem, man. No doubt about it. It's the pie. The fuckin pie.
An who sold the pie?

Mad Dog gives it to him straight. Gives it to him in no uncertain terms, man. Fed up fuckin about. Fed up pussyfootin. Tells the wee Luigi man that he caused it. Caused the problem. Caused him all the soapybubble. Aye, Mad Dog wants squared up. Wants compensated.

C'mon, pay up ya wee cunt. Play the fuckin white, man. Fair's fair.

The wee man's eyes pop. Mouth drops. He's pure stunned. Aye, really taken aback, so he is. Ah mean, how the fuck could anybody suggest his pies were foosty. Best fuckin food in the town. Check the window. Aye, it says it loud an clear.
The bold Luigi starts gettin stroppy. Really fuckin peeved, man. Ah mean, his pies foosty? No way José. No fuckin way. It's an insult. A right slap on the tits, so it is.

He starts swearin. Not swearin as in fuckin, cuntin, bastart type swearin. Naw, he starts swearin on his a-Mama-mia, on-a-leetle-a-bambinos, on-a-sacred-a-heart-a-da-Jesus, Luigi-no-sell-a-da-dodgy-pie-man. Luigi-pie-a-best-in-a-business. He claims Big Chucky boy was blitzed out his face. Fuckin rat-arsed. Aye, too much a-da-dreenk. Da-dreenk-fuck-up-a-da-belly.

Mad Dog's had it, man. Had it up to here. Fuck sake, tryin to be nice, tryin to be mister nice guy givin cunts a break an what do ye get, man? This. This shit.

This big fuckin paw comes crashin down on the counter. Everythin shudders. Fish n chips n pies n sausages do somersaults. Wee Luigi's eyeballs lan on the counter an his sphincter muscles are bleetin ten-a-penny.

Oky-da-doky, the wee man goes. Aw, pleeze-a-for-fuck-sake-no-wreck-a-ma-shop.

He tells us we can scran up, man, it's on the house. Free meal free drink.

Take-a-da-pick, he says, pointin to the stuff sizzlin away. Whatcha-da say?

Mad Dog rolls back the bottom lip an nods slow. Says, Deal.

Deal, Luigi goes.

Is it? Is it a deal?

Listen, ah'll tell ye this for fuck-all. Tarmen are greedy cunts with big fat bellies. An as ye well know by now, Mad Dog's a fly cunt.
He orders up a special fish supper with loads of salt n vinegar, two pickled onions, a pickled egg, two rolls n butter, a king size Mars Bar, a packet of cheese n onion, a bottle of Irn-Bru an forty Club King-size.
It's much the same all round, man. Every cunt gets wired in. Grub, fags, ginger. Anythin ye fuckin like, help yerself, it's on the house.

An wee Luigi seems quite happy, so he does. Ah mean, the wee cunt can't grumble, can he? Naw, he's not been knocked out or had his shop turned over or had to part with any cash. Well, anyway, it comes round to Big Chuck's turn.
Big Chucky boy. Relief screemin out him. Aint gonni get a kickin. An it's his turn to pick, man. Aye, take yer pick.
Wee Luigi man asks him, What-a-da-ya-want?

He still feels peely-wally but. Still got a dodgy New Delhi. Still a wee bit nippy-arsed. Could mibbee try just a wee nibble but, eh? Just a wee bite. After all, it's a freebie fuck.

He saunters over slow. Clocks the grill. Aw, man, don't the big

guy's eyes just come alive. Aw, check the fuckin scran. Fish an chips an black puddins an pies all sizzlin an cracklin away. Ain't that just sweet music to yer tonsils.
Big Chucky boy. What the fuck's he like? Old Scrooge himself feastin the peepers on a pot of gold.

Can't make his mind up. Can't.
Big cunt just stood an stared for ages.
Then he went an done it. Aye.
D'ye know what the big bastart went an done next?
Swear to fuck, man, wait till ye hear this. Ye'll never believe it if ye live till yer ninety.
He fuckin starts hummin an hawwin.

Aw, fuck, can't pick, can't pick, can't make the auld mind up, he goes. How the fuck ye meant to pick, eh? Yer spoilt for choice, man int'ye?
Aw, fuck, eh... ah'll have a... eh ah'll have a... eh... can't make the auld mind up, man. Ah think ah'll have a... a...
Fuck it, man, ah'll tell ye what ah'll have. Ah'll have another steak pie supper.

Honest to fuck, by the way, that's what the big daft bastart went an done.
Aye. Swear it, man. After all that. That's what the big cunt done.

Chapter Eight.
The Stop n Go.

Right wait till ah tell ye about the auld Stop n Go. Aw, for fuck sake, man.

The dreaded Stop n Go.

It's a job made in hell, so it is. Ye just stan there like a numpty with yer red n green lollypop an listen to nothin but absolute dog's abuse. Fuck me, man, ye want to hear it.

Ye take more shit than a fuckin septic tank, honest. Even the auld village idiot rips the pish out ye.

Ye want to hear Joe Public in their motors. C'mon to fuck, they shout, ah've these kids to get to school an ah'm half an hour late for my work as it is, ya fuckin half wit ye. Ye've had that board at Stop for donkeys.

An then there's the heavy team. The hairy-arsed lorry drivers. Gonni knock yer cunt in, gonni ram yer daft big sign right up yer arse, wrap it round yer neck, stuff it down yer throat. Aye, if ye keep them waitin one more second that's what they're gonni do, they shout.

An ah'll tell ye another thing.

Burds? Ye've not got a snowball's chance in Hell of gettin a burd once ye've worked the Stop n Go. The minute yer han touches that board ye've had it. The world's biggest wanker has a better chance than you have boy, ah'm tellin ye. Yer fuckin finished. Finito.

As soon as ye see a bit of fanny comin ye start cringin, so ye do. Aye, ye feel the auld boat race blazin like a steelwork furnace.

Aw, fuck fuck fuck fuck fuck, man, what ye gonni do, eh, eh?
What the fuck ye gonni do?
Hide?
Where? Ye can't, man, there's no fuckin hidin place. Naw. Ye
just stan there rooted to the spot, scarlet, just holdin yer big
bright red n green lollipop an wish ye could hide yer head
up yer arse.

Ye stan there an suffer, watchin them walk by, wigglin their
tight little arses in their tight little mini skirts an they point an
whisper an giggle an ye know they'll tell all their mates an
that'll be it, man. Fucked. Yer finished. Ye'll never ever ever
ever ride another burd again, so ye won't. Never. Ah'm tellin
ye, see even if ye live till yer ninety, ye'll be known forever as
the lollipop man.
Aw, my Christ. The lollipop man. The fuckin party's over, ah'm
tellin ye.
Names stick so they do. Nicknames stick.
But that's not the worst thing. Naw. The worst thing's the cold.

Jeeezazzz.

Pile on the clobber. Pile it on. Balaclava, tammy, thermal
semmit, three tee-shirts, two jumpers, body warmer, donkey
jacket, long johns, two pairs of joggers, two pairs of socks an
yer big beefy toe-tectors.
Ye pile the fuckin lot on, the works. An ye stan there all nice
an cozy, so ye do. Snug as a bug in a rug. Aye, for what? Ten,
fifteen, twenty minutes tops?
An then slowly it hits ye. It's light at first, so it is. Like a soft
cool breeze ticklin the tip of yer skin. But then it starts pressin
in slowly, gettin tighter n tighter. A slight nip. Sting.

The nose, man, aye, it's the tip of the nose ye feel first. Then

fingers an toes. Piercin in sharper an sharper. This numbin ache
bitin the base of yer back eatin its way up to the nape of yer
neck. Aye, yer neck. Aw, yer poor fuckin neck, man.
Listen close an ye'll hear it grindin. Grindin like nails down a
blackboard as all day long yer head turns left right left right
left right left left right left right left right left right left right
left right left right left right.

All day long, man. Left right left right left right.
Watchin all the traffic. People's faces. Angry pissed-off faces
lookin down their noses.
An ye just stan there an turn yer lollipop.
Turn it to Go. Turn it to Stop.
Stop Go Stop Go Stop Go Stop Go Stop Go Stop Go Stop Go.

Aw my fuck, man. The dreaded Stop n Go. A job made in Hell.
Designed by the Devil.
Not a cunt in the whole wide world'll touch it by the way.
Ah'm tellin ye, no cunt.

Hey, no cunt that is, except Bobo.
Aye, our Big Bobo. Bobo's yer man. Loves, it so he does. Aye,
the auld Stop n Go suits the big filla mighty fine.
Ah'll tell ye why.
Big Bobo's deaf. Honest. Deaf as a deck of cards.
See all that shoutin n bawlin an, Haw, dickhead, ah'll ram that
board right up yer arsehole. Easy meat for the big yin.
Shout all the fuck yees like, cunts. Bobo boy's oblivious. Fuck-
all to Bobo.

An ah'll tell ye another reason it suits him. He's twenty-two
stone. Twenty-two stone if he's an ounce, right?
So any heavy graft's down the shitter. Can't do it. No chance.
Big guy walks ten yards an he's blowin like a fuckin sperm

whale. Billions of little bloodworms bustin out his big burgundy boat race.

So fuck that work stuff. No-can-do-man, can't be done. Can't. Naw. Can't rake, shovel, chip, or brush even. Naw, the big cunt can't even brush.

Stop n Go for Bobo. Suits the big guy fine.

So like ah say, none of the troops would touch it. Hey, watch yerself boys, there's shite on the hanle of that lollipop, they'd shout.

Honest, man, ye'd gladly stan buried up to yer waist in shite before ye'd touch the auld red n green chappy. Aye, standin on yer head too.

That was until. Until.

One day the auld Stop n Go went hi-tec.

Lollipop no more. Naw. Now it's a fancy machine. Digital. No more standin there with the blue bollocks n crimson face.

Now ye sit down. Take a wee pew, man, relax.

Sit where ye like. Sit in the hut n have a smoke. Stick the kettle on.

Put the feet up, man. Toast the auld plates of meat at a nice hot fire an watch the cars go by an the men at work knockin their cunts in.

Nice wee neat gadget sittin on yer lap. Two buttons.

Big remote control board, just turns itself.

Stop Go Stop Go.

Two buttons, man. Two wee buttons. Red button green button.

Stop Go Stop Go. Fuckin dawdle. Easy life.

Well now all of a sudden it's a good job, innit? Now it's the fuckin berries. Every cunt an their dog wants a shot.

Gonni gimmee a shot big yin, eh? Just a wee shot. Aw, go'n,

go'n. Let me get a blow, eh? A wee smoke. Aw, go'n for fuck sake, man. Ten minutes.

Bobo boy's havin none of it. No way, man, no way José.
Big guy's like a pig in a dung heap. Ah'm tellin ye. H A P P Y.
Mad Dog can't wait, man. Dyin for a wee shot so he is. What's he like? Like a tranny at an Anne Summers night.
Tea-time, Mad Dog signals to Bobo. That's it, tea-time. Points down the road. Tells Bobo to take a break. Points at the gadget. Gimmee a wee shot.

Mad Dog's on the machine. The fancy machine. Bobo's pride n joy.
Sittin there. Thumb twiddlin, watchin the cars goin by.
Sittin pressin buttons. Press the Stop button press the Go button.
Press Stop Go Stop Go Stop Go.

This is the life, man. Pure dead brilliant.

The auld sign's birlin like a ballet dancer. Mad Dog's on fire.
Havin a ball like a nymph at an orgy.
Fuck it, he goes, payback time. Time to cause chaos.
Time to show the bastarts who's boss.
Aye, yer man's fed up listenin to shite. Time to strike a blow for the little chappies. Y'know what ah'm sayin? Time to put a stop to all this haw-arsehole-turn-that-fuckin-board patter.
Aye, all yer haw-you-ah've-been-waitin-this-long-waitin-that-long's gettin knocked on the head right now, so it is. Aye, right this minute.
Fuck it, yer man's had enough, had it up to here.
Fuck em all. Take shit from no, man.
He hides behind the hedges pointin the gadget at the sign.
Round it goes, birlin away itself with not a cunt in sight.

Stop Go Stop Go.

Well, talk about curiosity killin cats.
What about curiosity crashin motors? Aye, all the curious cats
driving past with the mouths hangin open watchin it birlin
away an nobody's near it. Nobody. What the fuck's goin on?
Check the look on their faces. STRANGE.
Well, ye see, they aint watchin are they? Naw, not watchin the
road ahead, too busy ogglin away at this magic sign birlin
round stoppin an startin the traffic.
Stop start stop start an not a soul in sight.
Aye, they're so tranced up the cunts ain't watchin the road an
don't realise that they're a midge's baw hair away from the car
in front's arse.

Ye want to see the faces on the fuckers when they realise.
Honest. Pure picture. The auld eyebrows go V-shaped an the
eyeballs an mouth just spread out, so they do. Ye see their skin
stretchin like an Olympic sprinter doin a hundred mile an hour
into a strong wind. Ye know what ah mean? Aye, their auld
faces take on that melted plastic look an their heads disappear
inside their necks an their whole body shoots forward as they
ram the gutty down on the brakes.
Phew, fuck me, man, that was close. Sometimes they make
it, just stoppin in time, just missin the guy in front's arse
by inches.
Aye, sometimes. But hey, sometimes they don't.
Listen. It gets better. Aye, the best laugh's when the big artics
trundle up. Thirty ton of metal forty-foot long, with some fat
prick behind the wheel in a tartan shirt an denim cap givin it
the gutty.
He sees this the big sign. Bright green background with big
white letters.

Clear as ye like. Can't miss it.

GO

Through he comes. Mad Dog lies there waitin. Waitin. Nice an easy now, got to get it right. Timin, it's all in the timin. Can't be too early, can't be too late.
Fifty yards, forty yards, thirty, twenty, ten.
Bingo.
Press button. Sign turns.

STOP

The big Yorkie man's face, check the look on the fucker's face. Pure shock horror panic. His size sixteen feet hit the floor an the wagon folds in the middle. it's jack-knifin.
It slithers like a sidewinder right across the street with its brakes squeelin like a pig in a gang bang an its engine whinin louder than a jumbo jet.
An waftin up through tall this is the stench of burnin rubber.
An shite.

Aye, shite. There's this right gaggin smell of shite comin from the cabin.
Check the big Yorkie man now. Tough guy. Same big guy that was gonni ram signs up people's arseholes an break things over people's backs.
Aye, gonni do this, gonni do that.
Heh, don't fuck with the Crazy Gang, Mad Dog's Crazy Gang, big rough tough Yorkie man.
Look at ye now, eh. Look at ye, standin there with the shite runnin down yer leg. Ain't so smart now are ye?

An there's not a thing he can do about it, man. Naw, nothin. Not a fuckin thing.

He just sits there scratchin his big sweaty shite-caked arse an lookin at this sign birlin round an round an not a soul in sight. Just Mad Dog hidin in the bushes, rollin about pishin his pants laughin.

Chapter Nine.
2 dummies? Naw, 3.

Next thing we know the Polis appear. That's what happens with Polis, innit? They appear.

Mad Dog always hated Polis. Used to wind them up like fuck, so he did, loved nothin better than rippin the pish right out their arses.
Used to walk up to them an go, How come you cunts always wear the exact same gear, eh? How'd yees know what the other one's wearin?
Bet yees phone each other up the night before, he'd go. Aye, bet yees phone each other up an say, Hey, what are we wearin tomorrow? Short-sleeve shirts? Aye, fine. What about Wednesday? Think we'll go for woolly jumpers on Wednesday. Right, no probs. Aw listen, what d'ye fancy wearin next week on night shift? Ah was just thinkin it's ages since we both went out wearin our overcoats. Overcoats? Aye well, OK, overcoats it is then.

Ye want to have seen the faces on the Polis when he said that to them. Should've seen the look they gave him.
Told him to get to fuck, so they did. Aye, they went like that, Get yersel to fuck right now ya big screwball or ye'll be down that road in two seconds.

Aye, so anyway, the Polis appear on the job an walk over. One middle-aged, slight paunch, wearin the auld can't-be-bothered look. Been in the service twenty years an just bidin his time kinda thing, tickin off the days. Aye, he's well set up for the auld early retirement lark. Hansome lump sum, tidy weekly pension. Can't wait can't wait.

The other dude. Young an hansome keep-fit type. Plays squash, lifts weights, spends ten nights a week on the sunbed an uses two tubs of gel on the hair.

He's one of yer look-at-me-I'm-a-right-cool-fucker-too-cool-for-this-uniform-shit-I-should-be-a-super-cool-plain-clothes-detective-like-the-ones-you-see-on-telly type of cunt.

Crime-buster. Gonni kick ass.

Inside the plooky-arsed prick there's this a Detective Chief Inspector screamin to get out.

Fat Head an Pretty Boy. Usual combo.

Fat Head starts spielin it off to Bobo. Tellin him he's in serious shit. Violation of this Traffic Act, that Traffic Act, breach of Chapter this an Chapter that. Says there's all sorts of reports comin in. Reports of him almost causin an accident.
Causin, not preventin, a fuckin accident.

Serious shit son, he says to Bobo. Need to take you down the Station.
Bobo just throws him that vacant look. Shrugs an turns the palms out an points to the ears. Opens the auld mouth dead wide an goes, Deahh duhh naww speeee.
Tries like fuck to talk, man. He nearly chokes tryin to make words. Fuckin sin.

The two Coppers clock each other. The penny drops. Cleeeenk, cleeeenk, cleeeenk. Fuckin hell. A dummy.
The name-a-fuck, what are they like, eh? Check the faces.
A pure picture. Any cunt got a camera?
Fat Head starts talkin slow. Mouth wide open. Aye, he starts

talkin like Bobo. Whoooo's iin chaaaaaarge.

Bobo points across at Mad Dog.

The Polis pull Mad Dog.

Well, as you an I well know, the bold Mad Dog's a shrewdy. He's been watchin this all along. Seen what's happenin. Got it well-sussed.

Starts shruggin an pointin to the ears an mouth givin it, Deahhh, duhhh, nawww speeeee.

Throws it on heavy too, lettin the tongue hang out. Starts doin the sign lingo, twiddlin the fingers.

The two Polis're well scoobied, so they are. The auld heads are welded right up their arses.
They start whisperin. Aye, they start this daft whisperin out the sides of their mouths.

Turn round, Fat Head goes. Turn yer back, these cunts can lip-read.

What're we gonni do? he says to Pretty Boy. Can't take them down the Station. Ye need to get an interpreter for a start. Then ye need to make phone calls, go through channels, follow fancy procedures. Ye'd write off a rainforest with all the paper-work that's needed. We'd be there all fuckin night, an me an the good lady's goin out. Been promisin her for weeks too, aye, told her to get a wee make-over an a new dress. She's gonni get all dolled up, man, fair lookin forward to it, so she is. Might even get ma hole. Fuckin months since ah've had the auld Nat King, so it is.
An goin down to the Station with two dummies, for fuck sake. Ah mean, ye know the fuckin slaggin ye'll get.

Pretty Boy's in a hurry too. Says he can't hang about all night. Says it's the first weekend off in yonks, man, him an the troops are goin out on the town hittin the trendy nightspots, gonni spend the weekend ballin some gorgeous chicks.

Mad Dog's standin listenin. Big man's on fire. Big ragin bull. Fuckin dirty bastarts, he's sayin under his breath. Can't be bothered, eh? Too much hassle, innit? Aw, an the auld wife might get angry, might not let you near her wrinkly pussy, might end up not gettin yer hole all because of two dummies, eh? Aye, the bastarts might get slagged off down at the Station an fuckin tight-arsed Pretty Boy here has got all these young chicks lined up just waitin to be balled.

Ballin chicks!!!
Mad Dog hates cunts that talk like that. Red mist's comin down. Got to hang on but, can't give the game away now. Nearly there, man, nearly there.

The two Polis are still whisperin away. Still got their backs turned.
Fat Head goes, We'll just give them a warnin, then? Ah mean, the job's nearly finished by the looks ah things. Aye, a wee tellin off'll do the trick. We'll tell them we're reportin it to their high heidyins down the road an we're gonni be watchin them like fuckin hawks. Tell them we'll be makin regular checks an all that shit. Aye, that'll do it.

Fat Head comes over an starts layin down the law, tellin them how lucky they are. Aye, yees are a pair ah lucky laddies gettin let off so light, he tells them. Tells them they're lucky not to be gettin charged. Says he could've huckled them down the Station an stuck them in the cells for the night. Up in front of the Judge first thing. Mibbee even end up gettin jailed.

Aye. A pair ah lucky laddies.

Pretty Boy's noddin. Smilin away. Well pleased. Doesn't need all this shit. Ah mean, it ain't macho, is it? Couldn't impress the pussy with this story.

Aw, sorry I missed the party, girls, I spent all night down the Station chargin these two deaf mutes.

No way, man. Wouldn't do. Wouldn't do at all. Wouldn't go down well, doesn't fit with all his macho-man shit about trackin down gun-runners an bustin drug barons. Oh fuck naw, man.

Look at Mad Dog n Bobo. What are they like? Hans behind their backs, heads bowed, wee sad eyes. Two scolded school-boys. They both nod. They've got the message.
A pair ah lucky laddies.
But Mad Dog can't let it go. Can't leave it at that. Naw, the cunt's always got to push his luck. Always pushes it too far. Loves playin to the crowd, so he does. Nothin better than a bit of the auld showboatin. Loves stickin it right up the Polis. Fuckin loves it. He starts wavin the finger at Bobo. Teacher to schoolboy.
Starts twiddlin the fingers givin it heavy dummy lingo pointin to the board an turnin it to Stop turnin it to Go. Pointin at his eyes an pointin at the traffic.

Waaaghh duuurrgh dduu neeeu uughh, aye, pay attention you ya cunt, he's tellin him.

Turns to the Polis, starts shakin their hands, pattin their arms, Durrrghh daaawwwrrg geeerghhhk uhhhdd, he goes, pointin back at Bobo, wavin the big fist. Mad Dog winks at Bobo an salutes the Polis. Aye, fuckin salutes. Pushin it.

The big bastart's pushin it.
Bobo's drawin him daggers. His arse is sweatin, Big cunt's
gonni stick us in the shite, he's thinkin.

Fuck it, why worry? Bobo needn't worry, man. Deaf as a steel
toe-cap. Nothin to hide. Eezy peezy, man. Dawdle.

Look at the Polis. Check the faces. What are they like? Chuffed
to bits, so they are. Aye, problem solved. All in a day's work,
eh?
We stan an watch as they head back to the Panda.
Mad Dog's cursin them like fuck under his breath.

Ya pair ah bastarts, ye can hear him sayin. Fuck yees. Go'n ya
fat auld cunt, away home to yer withered auld wife. Aye, bet
she's a picture. Bet ye, eh? Fuckin varicose-veined tits hangin
way down each side of her belly button an an auld crusty
fanny. Aye, an ye might even get yer hole too, ya auld prick.
Lucky bastart. Wish ah was you.

An what about young Pretty Boy? Check him out, man, what's
he like?
His arse is playin buttons, so it is. Hurry up, man hurry up, get
the boot down. Home shite shower shave. Hit the town, man,
hit the wine bars down Trendyville an chat up the chicks
with the fancy stories. Macho-man stories about rapists an
murderers an how they're all behind bars an the world's a
safer place. Oh yes. The world's now a much safer place to
bring up your children thanks to super-hero macho-man.
Macho-man. Sure. Gonni ball some chicks. Yeah yeah.

That's another thing. YEAH. Mad Dog hates cunts that say
YEAH.

Yeah, gonni ball chicks. Ball chicks. All weekend ballin chicks.

Aye, well, fuck you, ya bastart. YEAH.

We jump up an down doin back flips n front flips n
sommersaults n cartwheels. Every cunt's right out it, man. Ya
fuckin beauty.
Happy-heads all round. Every cunt's happy.
Every cunt bar Bobo. Aye, ye see, they don't like that. Don't
like ye doin their dummy lingo. Don't like cunts doin it just for
the sake of takin the piss. That's the way they see it like,
y'know? Takin the piss. Mad Dog was takin the fuckin piss.
Aye, big Bobo boy took the hump with Mad Dog.

Fuck him, Mad Dog says, fuck him. Can't say nothin, can he?
Ha ha ha. Can't say nothin. Get it?

Mad Dog thought that was a cracker. Can't say nothin.

Every cunt laughed. Every cunt bar Bobo.

Mad Dog was made up, man. He'd got one over the auld Polis.

Or so he thought. Ye see, sometimes yer past comes back to
haunt ye.
We're down the boozer this night. Karaoke. Ever heard Mad
Dog singin? Ever heard a cat with its balls caught on a fence?
Ah'm tellin ye, man. Fuckin murder.
He loves it. Karaoke daft. Thinks he's Elton John Elvis Presley
Michael Jackson Frank Sinatra Barry Manilow Buddy Holly
Rod Stewart Billy Joel David Bowie rolled into one.
He struts into the boozer like a superstar givin it, Ah suppose
yees'll be wantin a song then?

He doesn't ask. Naw. Just tells the guy. Just shouts over to him,
Haw, you stick my fuckin name up, ya cunt.

Wait till later on but, he says. Aye, wait till the place fills up.

A multi-talented artiste like yer man here needs a big audience.

There's this guy called Shug Wilde. The Super Karaoke King DJ. Honest to fuck, by the way, ye have to see this to believe it. The wee pencil moustache pointy side-burns an the palm tree shirt.
Ye know what ah'm talkin about, right? Wanker.

Terrified of Mad Dog, so he is. Scared shitless. As soon as Mad Dog crosses the door the Shug fella's over like a shite off a hot shovel givin it, Oh gonni sing this one gonni sing that one, oh ah think yer absolutely fabulous at that one, oh honest to God big guy ah really can't make my mind up what one yer the most fabulous at.

Mad Dog hates him back. Hates him with a fuckin vengeance. Don't get me wrong he loves all that arse-lickin routine. Aye, he laps that up, but he hates yer man Shug. Always gonni kill the cunt, knock him out, bury the bastart. Ye want to hear him when he starts.

Ah'm gonni bury that bastart, he'll go. Fuckin knock him out, bang bang bang bang, teach the cunt a lesson, teach him not to make a fool of yer man, so ah will.

Mad Dog had it in for him ever since that incident with Angie. Classic so it was. Did ye not hear about it?
Wait till ah tell ye what happened.

Mad Dog fancied Angie. Used to fantasise like fuck about her. Ye want to have heard him when he got started. Bet ye her pussy's tighter than two coats of paint, he used to say. Bet she shaves it too, aye, just leaves a wee drop to tickle yer hooter when yer yoddlin up her canyon. Aye, picture it, man. Bet ye it'll have a wee Hitler moustache on it. Bet ye her fuckin nipples are like football studs too, aye, hang a soakin wet duffle coat on them, so ye could. Aw, man, picture her in thigh-length leather boots with fishnet stockins an a wee leather G-string cuttin up her crack, an one of those wet look PVC basques. Fuckin hell, man, picture it picture it. Imagine her standin there with the auld whip in the hand lettin rip. Whoooosh, smack, man, fuck ye, right across the cheeks of yer arse with it, an then jumpin all over yer back with those big stiletto heels, eh? Aw, yes yes yes hurt me baby hurt me, give me some more of that gorgeous pain.

Aye, that's the way he used to rant n rave. Used to get carried away, so he did. Liked to give it the right heavy-duty droolin at the mouth stuff.
So anyway, this night he's doin a bit of the auld chantin, the usual pullin the place down stuff. He's every cunt's hero an the auld adrenalin's pumpin like a hard-core porn star. Angie looks well impressed. Standin there posin like fuck, man, tits bustin out her blouse, skin-tight mini-skirt half-way up her arse.

Mad Dog can't stand it, can't hold back no longer. She's after him, after his body.

After ma body, he goes. She's fuckin gaggin for it, so she is, gaggin for it. Ye can tell a mile away. Look, look at the size of those pupils, look at them. Fuckin pin heads. That's how ye know by the way, wee pupils means they're horny. Ah mind readin it in some scud book.
So this is it, he's thinkin. Go for it. Tonight's the night.

He sticks the chest out an struts over an leans into her ear. There's a right cunt of a racket goin on so he's got to shout loud.

He shouts, Angie babe, who's seein ye home tonight darlin, who's the lucky guy?

Well ye know what Angie's like, don't ye? Real slut but thinks she's a lady. Talks that hoity-toity posh way. Ooooh, ah love me, who do you love? She looks about to see who's watchin. Forces out a slight blush an gives the big eyelashes a flutter. Mad Dog's waitin. Strainin his lugs through the noise, gaggin for the right answer.

You, she goes.

Aw, yes, man, yes. Mad Dog's whoopin it up. Fuckin cracked it. He's beamin, so he is, beamin. Can't wait to tell the troops. Cracked it boys, ah'm tellin yees, he's goin. Just asked her who's seein her home. D'yees know what she said? D'yees fuckin well know what she said?
YOU, she says. YOU. Yours fuckin truly here's seein her home. Aye, honest. She's gaggin for it. Couldn't fuckin wait for me to ask her. Says she thought ah'd never ask. Ah'm tellin yees, troops, she's been eyein up yer man for yonks. Been givin the big guy the come-on.

Mad Dog's prick's explodin out his jeans. Gonni do all sorts of dirty stuff to Angie. Gonni fuckin lick her out, gonni ram it down her throat, gonni ram it up her jacksie, gonni do this, do that, do the next thing. Can't wait can't wait can't wait. Nearly shootin his load just talkin about it. Doin every cunt's nut in, so he is.
Anyway, the end of the night comes an every fucker an their dog's standin watchin. Mad Dog slings on the jacket, sticks out the chest an struts over cool-cat style.
No cunt can believe it, man. What the fuck's it like, eh?
Mad Dog an Angie. Beauty an the beast.

Let's go, baby, he says. Let's go. Your place or mine?

She looks at him. Looks him up an down like he's covered in shite. Tells him straight, tells him she's going home with HUGH.

Aw, holy fuck, man, HUGH. She said HUGH not YOU. Mad Dog thought she said YOU, didn't he? Aye, well ah mean, come on to fuck, man, how many Shugs do you know that get called Hugh, eh?

Well that was it. Big Mad Dog's face went redder than a worm-infested baboon's arse. Ye should've seen it. Ah'm telling ye by the way, it was like a fuckin red sky in the mornin shepherd's warnin. It was that colour.
He started growlin like a gorilla with a migraine.

Fuckin Hugh, eh? Hugh? Ah'll fuckin Hugh, the bastart. Ah'll give him Hugh. Fuckin teach the cunt to make a fool of me. Gonni knock the cunt out, man, give him the one two one two bang bang bang bang, two upstairs two downstairs, fold him like a tuppenny book, the bastart. Aye, Shug Wilde, Super Karaoke King DJ.

So anyway, where was ah? Aye, the bit about yer past comin back to haunt ye.
Right, we're down the boozer an it's Karaoke night an Mad Dog's up chantin, givin it big licks. He's pullin the place down, whoopin the ladies into a frenzy.
This is one for the ladies, he shouts.
Aye, auld fogies an drunken sluts with splungy knickers scream their fuckin heads off.
Mad Dog's givin it Clapton.

Shug Wilde's givin it the thumbs up, man. Can't wait for Mad Dog to finish so he can tell him how magic he was an buy him a drink an tell him how he's wastin his time here an that he should be on a bigger stage an that his talents know no bounds an he's born for greater things.

But there's this cunt at the bar. Dunno what the fuck he's all about, man. He's one of these well-to-do mature types. Looks right out of place in here, ah'm tellin ye.

Mad Dog clocks him. Starts watchin him an wonderin who he is. Agent maybe? Talent spotter out doin the rounds hopin to get lucky. Hopin to maybe stumble on the auld goose with the keks down layin that great big golden egg.
He's takin a big interest in Mad Dog. Fuckin peerin at him through slitty eyes that give that ah've-seen-you-somewhere-before-but-ah-can't-think-where look.

Mad Dog's playin to the crowd thrustin the hips an squeezin hard on the crotch givin it pelters.

He shouts at the crowd
Get up oan yer feet!

Aw, he's feelin high as a coke-head, man. He's cracked it. This is it. This is the breakthrough. The big one. The big apple, the one he's been waitin for all his days. The bold Shug was right enough, fuckin absolutely brilliant magic wonderful amazin voice, man, too good for this place.
The bold Shug knows his stuff. Not a bad cunt.

The dude starts natterin to Dave the barman.
Starts pointin up at Mad Dog, shruggin his shoulders, noddin his head an then shakin his head slow. He's givin it a fuckin-can't-believe-it-this-guy's-too-good-for-this-place type of shake. Dave's doin the same. Noddin, shakin, pointin at Mad Dog an smilin.

Mad Dog's goin for broke. Big gran finale. Crescendo.

His deep husky vocals rip through the rafters.

The whole place erupts, man, all the auld fogies are liftin their kilts an showin off big fuckin damp patches on the crotches of their bloomers. Drunken whores howkin up the pussy pelmets an runnin to the lavvy an smearin on the ruby red lipstick. Oh fuck aye, man, they're all squirtin a wee jag of bootleg perfume down the gusset an smearin a wee blob of vaseline on the sphincter lips. Mad Dog's in town.

Shug Wilde's shot his load. Goin all white an light in the head. He stays conscious long enough to do his, Aw-my-God-aw-my-God-Mad-Dog-Mad Dog-that-was-fuckin-abolutely-awesome-best-yet-absolutely-wonderful what-a-fuckin-talent-too-good-for-this-place performance.

The talent scout type's gone. Where?
Where's he gone, man? Out to the car mibbee, eh?
Aye, out to get the forms for yer man to sign. Here ye are, sign here big boy, fifty gran up front an a gran a night plus all ye can drink with gang-bangs galore for you an all yer buddies laid on in the deal.

This is it, man. This is it. Mad Dog's arrived.

Show-time.

He rushes over to Dave.
Wants to know who he was. The dude. The talent scout guy.
Who was he? What was he? What did he want, eh? Mad Dog's desperate to know.

Was he after me? Was he? Was he? Was he?
Was he chasin me up, eh? eh? eh? eh?

Dave the Rave worked in London for a week once. Ye want to hear the state of the big cunt talkin.
He starts tellin Mad Dog the full story. Aw, for fuck sake, man, ye want to hear this.

Yeah, he goes, fackin ryght ee was chasin you up mate.
Fackin cant was givin ya thee eye, so ee wos. Says ee could swear im an is china cautioned two cants a few fackin months back. Says these pair ah cants were dummies, man. Yeah an then the cant starts givin it fackin evvy verbal, askin if you maybee ad an identical twin or wot?

Mad Dog's eyeballs pop out his head. His bottom jaw, hits the bar

CRUNCH.

Skin an bone go head-to-head with hard mahogany.
Hairline fracture.
Aw, fuck, man. Mad Dog's well rattled. A double whammy, eh?
A double downer. From riches to rags in seconds. Dreams of stardom wiped out faster than a white heavyweight. Aye, say ta ta to yer five star hotel. Hotel Barlinnie here we come. In the name ah fuck, man, the only gang bang material he'll get anywhere near now'll have a three-day growth an a big fat hairy arse.

Ah well, fuck it, Mad Dog shrugs. Why change the habits of a lifetime?

But then Dave the Rave looks at him an smiles, Hey, keep the fackin chin ap mate, fack me, ya don't fink I'd fack ya in tha shit mate. Fackin ell, wot fackin sort of a cant, dja fink I am? Na, jast fackin told thee old cant, fackin told im straight, mate, said, Listen you old fackin cant, there weren't fackin two dammies mate. Na, there was fackin three. Three fackin dammies. The fackin old cant keeps arpin on about there only bein fackin two, don't ee? Well, by this time I'm fackin losin the old fackin rag, aint I? Yeah. So I just turns an fackin gives it to im straight. Just fackin says to im, listen you old cant remember that big fackin twenty-two stone red-faced cant with the fackin arse like a fackin dabble-decker side-on? Yeah, well, that big cant was a dammy right? An you an yer poofy fackin prick-ed of a mate are a fackin pair ah dammies. Well that makes three fackin dammies in my fackin book, now don't it, cant? Now fack off.

Mad Dog smiles a big gap-toothed grin at Dave an asks him if he's brushed his teeth this mornin.

Tells him the reason he's askin is because he's just about to give him the world's fuckin biggest slabbbery kiss.

Chapter Ten.
Silky Sid an the prize bull knob.

Sid was a shirtlifter. Aye, big Silky. Silky Sid.
Poor big cunt thought nobody knew too. Naw, thought
nobody noticed.
Ah mean, as if ye wouldn't notice, eh?
The long nails, the soft hans, the theatrical expressions, the
walk, the talk. All that shit. Ah mean, yer not gonni blend in,
man. No way, not in here, not in this shit-hole. Somewhere
else mibbee, aye, like a hair salon in London or a fashion
boutique in San Francisco. But here for fuck sake, here? A
fuckin tar squad in Coatbridge. Do me a favour.

Strange.
Still, mibbee the poor cunt thought it would go away. Aye, just
vanish, just wake up one mornin an, fuck ye, ah'm normal.
Look at me ah'm normal, oh thank you Lord, thank you thank
you thank you.

Aye, mibbee that was it. Mibbee he thought he'd turn out like
us, eh? Rough an tough like us cunts, walkin about there
scratchin the balls, pickin the hooter, fartin, boakin, whistlin at
all the fanny. Oh fuck aye, bet ye he dreams about bein able to
do all that stuff, eh? Fuckin hell, man, Sid whistlin at the
fanny? Imagine.

Give him his due but, the big cunt just got on with it. He just
battered on. Just worked away an ignored cunts.
Or as ah say, he mibbee thought we never knew. Fuck.
Then one day it happened. Aye, it happened just like that. Ah
remember it well.

Sid. The bold Sid boy came out. Aye, out of the auld closet came Sid.
Well, he didn't so much come out, as was outed. Pushed rather than jumped, if ye get ma meanin.

It was big Hovis that caused it.
The big cunt just walked right into the canteen this day an went, Ken what Sid, just you go an work with big Chuck.

Honest to fuck, man, that's what he done. Sent Sid to work with Chuck. Fuck sake. Dunno if it was deliberate, man. Dunno. Ah mean, ye wouldn't think so. But then again, ye dunno with that cunt Hovis, so ye don't. Ye just can't tell. Sick sense of humour the big cunt's got.

Sid an Chuck. Fuckin lethal cocktail.

There's big Chucky boy. Y'know what he's like, man, ye'know what he's like. Big hairy chest, wee tight vest, tattoos, baseball cap an the big bulgin groin bustin through the skin tight jeans. Real Village People stuff.

Aw, for fuck sake, man. The Sid boy, what's he like?
Died an gone to heaven. Just standin there starin. Fuckin tongue hangin out, sweatin, sweatin, feelin faint, can't believe his eyes. Can't.
Big Chuck, man, fuckin gorgeous, aw, my God, gorgeous, aye, his dream boy, his fantasy lover, big Chuck, big rough tough construction worker Chuck, oh my God, oh my God. What's he like, eh? What's he like? Like somethin straight out a leather-joy-boy mag. Honest.

Well ye know the script with the Chucky boy don't ye.
Aye, his knob. His fuckin big prize bull knob. Talks about it non-stop, so he does. Non-stop.

Ma knob ma knob ma knob. That's all ye get, man.
Swear it. Mornin noon an night.
An it doesn't matter a fuck what the subject is, football, boxin,
politics, anythin. The big man'll get round to talkin about his
big knob with the veins on it like a bodybuilder's bicep.

Big Chuck Mcfuck. Jumpin about daft, squeezin his loins an
rantin an ravin.

Aye, stick my big knob in her so ah would, he'd go. Ah'm tellin
ye by the way, yer man here would have her screamin.
Screamin blue murder.
Give it to her it right in the divot, oh fuck aye. Here darlin,
impale yersel on this.

Big Chuck's squeezin the chomper an sayin to Sid, See this big
thing here, man, ah'm tellin ye, ah fuckin hang ma donkey
jacket on it when ah'm shavin so ah do. Aye, ah just stan an
shave away with the jacket hangin over ma knob.
Two pockets crammed with change too. Don't even know
it's there.

So Sid feels like he's gettin the come-on. Thinks big Chuck's
makin moves. Well, ye can't blame the poor cunt, ah mean the
average guy in the street doesn't stan there squeezin his balls
an give a runnin commentary on what he does with his hard-
ons now does he? Naw, not unless he's after somethin.

Aye, the big cunt must be after somethin, Sid thinks.

But he can't jump in. Naw, he can't, man, he's feart, he's too
feart. Easy does it, man, ye've got to go easy, so ye have. Ye
don't want to go divin in just in case yer wrong.
Big Chuck's still squeezin away.
Standin there leanin back, legs parted, chest out. Lappin up

the attention. Playin to the crowd. He can tell Sid's well impressed.

Hot-Rod they called me at school, he goes. See when ah was younger, ah could bend six inch nails round it, so ah could. Aye, big hard tungsten nails, right round it they'd go. Fuckin easy. Solid muscle.
Can't do it now but, naw, arthritis in ma wrists.
Aw, for fuck sake, man, ah'm tellin ye, eight inches sleepin, so it is. Eight inches from the bunnet to the scrotum.
An listen, hey, three an three quarter inch girth on it, man. Swear it. A peach, so it is. An absolute fuckin peach.
Ye want to see the head on the bastart, aw, man, listen, see when ah drag the auld skin back, we're talkin, aw, we're talkin about a fuckin sunrise here, aye, that's what springs to mind, man, honest.
All ah need to do is just give the shaft a wee squeeze to pump the blood through the veins an then slide back the skin an out she comes. Lights up the world so she does. Good mornin sunshine. Aw, man, ye want to see it.

Well that was it.
Sid's bleary-eyed an tremblin at the knees with the auld baw bag ready to bust all over the street.
His imagination's on fire. Honest to fuck, the auld imagination's goin haywire. He's got this picture. This vision of some kinda stone sculpture all tanned an oily.
Aye, the Sid dude sees Chuck's knob in his mind. A perfect picture, so it is. It's standin up stiff an rippled like a body-builder covered in bulgin blue veins. It has this glowing red head like the planet Mars.
Oh my God it's there, it's there, it's on a plate. The big man Chuck's put it on a plate. On a fuckin plate, man. Asked him

if he wanted to see, it so he did. Didn't he?

Fuck it, man, Sid can't stan it no longer. He's goin for it. The bold Siddy boy's goin for it. Can't fail, man. He can't. Big Chuck's given him the come-on. All the posin, flauntin, teasin. He's after his body. He must be.

Sid just comes out with it like that. Just asks big Chuck to show him his dick. Aye, starts talkin dead bitchy like, ye'know, layin on the heavy-duty poofy stuff. An posin. Posin like a fairy queen. Han on hip, fingerin the eyebrow.

Oooh la la big boy, Sid starts purrin.

He tells Chuck he can't get him out of his mind. Tells him he's his dream boy. Fantasy hunk. All that sort of stuff. Says he's got to see this big pork sword of his. Aye, can't wait no longer, man. Enough's enough. All the talkin's over. Time for action. Get it out big boy. Get it out now.

Sid tells him straight, man, tells him what he's all about. Says he'd crawl a mile of barbed wire for a glimpse. Says he'd gladly han over a tenner for a stroke at it.
Aye, a ten pound note's all yours, big boy, all yours. Just let me have a stroke. Oh yes yes yes, a long an gentle stroke, a soft an subtle caress, aw, please please please big boy, eh? Just you an me. Hows about it?

Well now. Well. Big Chuck, man, what's he like, eh?
His face is a pure picture. Doesn't know where to look. Starts seein red once it sinks in, once it really hits him what's happened. Fuck sake, just been accosted by this big poofy bastart. Big slate off the roof just asked to see his dick just like that. Right out the fuckin blue. Ah mean, all he was doin was talkin about it, that's all. Is a man not allowed to talk about his

dick in public, eh? Ah mean, his pride an joy. His big dick, his big precious dick for fuck sake. Ah mean, other people talk about things, don't they, their house, their car, their dog, their wife. Aye, everyday chit-chat, innit?

An offerin him money too. Fuckin offerin him money.
Big Chuck's mind's workin overtime, so it is. Doin twelve-hour shifts. What the fuck's he playin at, he's sayin to hisself. Big bastart must think ah'm a renter. Must think ah'm a fuckin rent boy, big cunt that he is. Ah'll show him, ah'll teach the poofy bastart a lesson.

Big Chuck sets about Sid. Pulls him down an starts jumpin all over his head. Does him right in, man, fuckin really wastes the poor cunt.

Ya big bastart, ya fuckin dirty big bastart, he's screamin, foamin at the mouth an callin Sid for everythin. Fuck ye, ya fairy-boy, try it on with me would ye, fuckin think ah'm a fruiter d'ye, eh? An offerin me money too. Ah'll fuckin teach ye, ya cunt that ye are, fuckin won't put a finger near ma dick so ye won't, no way, man, no way.

Sid, man. Poor big cunt's on the deck all curled up like a hedgehog an screamin the place down. Aye, screamin like a battered wife.
Big cunt had no chance, man. None. Fartin against thunder. Took a right hidin, so he did.
What a state. Face like a well-skelpt arse.
Pretty boy no more. Fuckin sin so it was. Liberty.

Mad Dog's beelin. Hates liberty-takers. He starts goin off his head at big Chuck. Starts callin him for everythin.

Ya dirty big bastart ye, that's right out of order.

Ah mean, hittin Sid? Imagine hittin that poor cunt, for fuck
sake. Aye, an for what, eh? For what? What did he do? Ask to
see yer dick? Was that it?
Where's the harm in that for fuck sake, all ye had to do was
say naw. That's all it takes, man. Ye didn't need to go an waste
the poor cunt.

Mad Dog's white, man. White. You always steer well clear
when he goes white.
He's starts proddin Chuck. Proddin his finger into his shoulder.

Show me yer dick, he goes. C'mon, big man, show's it, eh, let's
see how tough ye are now, c'mon. Hear what ah'm sayin,
d'ye hear? Why don't ye hit me then, eh? That's what ye do
when cunts ask to see yer dick don't ye, eh? That's what ye
normally do.

Chuck freezes.
Mad Dog's paw zips back. His arm's bent his hand's open. Big
back-hander on the way.
He holds it.
Holds it scorpion's tail style, steady, steady, ziiiiiiip, smack.
A light fleshy smack it makes, like a shit hittin bog water.
Nothin heavy, just a sting. Enough but. Enough.
Aye, enough to teach a lesson. No more bullying. No more
liberty takin.

So there ye are, man. That was how it happened. Big Sid
was out.
Out the closet. Every cunt in the town an their auntie knew.
Wasn't the best way for it to happen but. There must be an
easier way, eh? Must be.
Ah mean, normally when cunts are comin out they call a
wee meetin.

Family members only. Tell them all in private.
Fuck sake, ye don't want them findin out like this.

Aw, fuck, what a shock they'll get now, eh? A right bolt out
the blue this'll be. See once the auld tom-toms start beatin an
the tongues start waggin, the auld family'll get to hear about
it in no time. Aye, probably hear about it down the boozer or
down at the shops.

See yer son missus, he's a jobby-jabber so he is. Aye, he tried it
on with some laddie at work an got a severe kickin for it.
Quite fuckin right too.

Aw, for fuck sake, man. Poor Sid. Poor Sid was outed. An a
sore face to go with it. Aw, man. What mess.
What a fuckin mess.

We thought we'd never see him again. Honest. We thought
he'd han in his cards an fuck off down to London an never
come back.
But naw. Naw, naw. The Sids of this world are made of sterner
stuff. It's a fact. Once they're out they're out. That's it, man,
they get stronger, right? They take it on the chin, so they do.
Take all the hassle, all the names, gay, fruit-cake, nancy-boy,
queer. Aye, take it all in their stride an stick the finger up at
the world.
Before ye know it they start marchin through the streets in
their thousans givin it, Fuck yees fuck yees, I'm me, I'm a
human being, I have the same right as the next guy, the right
to choose, choose who I sleep with, choose who I gobble,
choose what shape of arse I want to fuck.
Aye, they start all that kinda shit. Start goin all aggressive,
man. Aye, the auld shy withdrawn frightened guy's out the
fuckin window. A new kid out the closet.

Well that was the case with our Sid. In fact it turned out Big Chuck had done him a favour. A real blessin in disguise, so it was. Cos see the followin day, sure as fuck, man, who struts right into the canteen but the right honourable Silky boy. Aye, honest. Just breezed in quite the thing.

But aw for fuck sake, man. His face. Ye want to have seen the state of his fuckin face. Could've put the Elephant Man on the burroo. Honest to Christ, by the way, ye'd swear he'd been skelpt with a fuckin double-decker.
Give him his due but, give the, man his due. He just marched right in, head up, chest out, I am who I am vibes screamin out him.

Fuck yees, he goes. Sticks the fingers up. Up yer arses.

Tension, man. Fuckin tension. Cut it with a chainsaw, so ye could. No cunt knows where to look.
Well fuck me with a rusty dildo, ye'll never believe what Mad Dog goes an does next.

Right up on the table he goes. Aye, jumps right up on the fuckin table an whups the dick out. Starts swingin it, man. Swingin it to-n-fro like a hypnotist's time piece.

Here ye are Sidney ma man, he goes. Get the tenner out an it's all yours. Do whatever ye fuckin like with it son. Look at it, stroke it, chew it, slap it off yer jaw. Do what ye like ma, man, just get the fuckin tenner out now. Ah'm yer man, aye, a tenner a stroke. Get right in there boy.

Well, the place just fuckin well explodes. Every cunt starts pissin their pants, man. Even Sid. Aye, the big cunt's face just brightens up like a starry night an he joins in laughin his arse off. Every cunt's laughin like fuck.

That was it, man. It broke the ice. The ice-breaker. Mad Dog the ice-breaker extraordinaire. Fair play, man. Fair dues.

Nobody bothered after that. Naw, no cunt bothered a fuck. We just let Sid be Sid.

An Chuck? Big cunt never mentioned his dick again. Well, not in front of Sid anyway.

Chapter Eleven.
Steamroom sweetie.

It stood Mad Dog in good stead, so it did. That carry-on with Sid. Ye know what they say, one good turn deserves another, an all that shit.

There was this cunt called Marcus Manley.
He'd cruise up in this big silver Shogun. Some machine, man, ye want to have seen it. Tinted windows, twin exhaust, blindin bright bull bars, the lot.
Pure dream machine.

Out he'd get, man, givin it the auld look-at-me-every-cunt-d'ye-know-who-ah-ahm-do-ye? Ah'm Marcus the man. Inspector Marcus Manley to you, cunt. Aye, show me some respect, show me some respect or yer done, out the game, finito.
One stroke of a pen an yer idle. Put ye on the buroo, so ah will. Marcus the man here'll put ye on the scoobie doo.

Fair dues but. As they say, if ye've got it made an livin on easy street, best of luck to ye.
Aye, the bold Marcus. Got it well made. Talk about cushy.
Struts his stuff, the bold Marcus struts his stuff. Check him out.
Whit's he like, whit the fuck's he like?
Aw, an ye want to have heard the shit the cunt talked. Fuckin bucketsful of the stuff.
Ah'm tellin ye by the way, half the lies the cunt told weren't true.
Honest, ye want to have heard these stories. An the thing is, ye had to stan an listen.
Up to yer knees in shit, listenin to the stories.

Jeezaz, man, ye want to have heard him.

Listen, he goes, Did ah tell yees this one, did ah, did ah tell yees?
Ah walks on to a job last, week so ah did. Should've seen their faces. These cunts thought they'd seen a ghost.
So ah just start shakin the head, don't ah. Start tellin them it won't do. No way José, won't do at all. Pre-coated chips are fuckin manky. Won't bind into the tar. Naw.
An another thing, there's not enough depth. Ah mean, ah'm lookin for sixty mill, minimum. Cunts have laid forty, tops. Fuck yees, ah go, out with it. Condemned.
Aw, honest to fuck, man, ye've seen ghosts with more colour in the auld cheeks, that's a fact.
Well the next thing the top, man goes an pulls me aside, right. Starts pleadin, so he does. Beggin for mercy. Starts spoutin all this shit about how this could finish him. He's fuckin rantin away about how he's only a small company livin on the breadline an times are real hard an he's only just stayin afloat an no more as it is an he's knockin his cunt in day in day out. Reckoned this could bury him. Aye, the prick was just about greetin.
Well, ah take him a walk across the street, don't ah. Aye, ah points in this shop window. There's this big paintin. Must be a fuckin gran's worth, easy. So ah goes like that to the cunt, See that big picture there? That would sure look nice above ma fireplace.
Aye, the bold Marcus gets bungs galore, man. Just like that. Turn a blind eye. Easy peezy, man. Doddle.

Mad Dog says, Fair dues, man. Best ah luck to ye. Good work if you can get it. Ah'd do the same maself in your shoes. Too right ah would. Too fuckin right.

Well that was all very well at first. Live an let live. But then he started gettin too big for his boots.

The Marcus man started to push his luck. Fuckin pushed it too far one day.

The cunt crossed the line. Started hasslin Mad Dog. Started comin up to the job givin it his auld shake of the head routine an tuttin away like an auld sweetie-wife. Aye, tuttin away so he was. Givin it, This'll no do an that'll no do. Ye know what ah mean? Nit pickin.

Sptarts pickin faults on the job sayin it's not rolled right. Yees haven't gave it enough rolls ya cunts, he'd go. Aye, he started talkin to us like that.

Ya cunts, he'd go, that job's not polished off, an those pre-coated chips're fuckin manky. They'll no stick. Naw, they'll no bind to the tar. An look at the state of those joints. They're no sealed right an they're hangin open like a whore's crack. The water'll seep under there. Aw, this'll no do. No do me at all. Fuckin out with it. Dig it out. Fuck yees.

Well, as ye can imagine, we were all dumbstruck. Why? Why was he doin it? What the fuck was the game, eh? Dunno. You tell me. Ah mean, what was he after? Money? Fuck sake, man, money off us cunts, are ye jokin? Favours? What could we do, what favours could we do Marcus? Give him a ride at Nancy, mibbee. Aye, take him up to the last house on the left. Marcus, meet Nancy. On ye go ma man, she's all yours. Go'n, get right in there with yer head down, she goes like a fuckin bunny.

Na, no chance.

Marcus wouldn't get his hans dirty, let alone his bollocks.

Turned out it was none of that. Naw. It was just an ego trip.
Just a big fuckin roller-coaster ego trip. Honest, that's what it
was all about. Just Marcus bein Marcus. Showin off an actin
the big shot, givin it heavy-duty swagger. Ah mean, ye've got
to put it about, no point in bein the big daddy an no cunt
knowin about it, is there? Got to press your authority, man,
got to lean heavy on the small people, remind them who's
boss, remind them that one snap of the fingers an one stroke
of the pen's all it takes.
Stroke of the pen an yees are finished, ya cunts. Wiped out.
Aye, that's what it was all about. Marcus the man. The boss
man puttin it about.

Dig it out, ya cunts yees. Fuckin dig it out.

Aw, in the name ah fuck. Mad Dog flung a king-size wobbler.
Never forget it, never. The look on his face, man. His eyes were
like burnin ice. Glassed over. Starin, just starin at nothin. They
say it all too, don't they? The eyes mirror the soul, so they say.
Aye, all that shit.

Mad eyes screamin blue murder.
It's a bastart when he goes like that. A cunt, man, a pure cunt.
Ah mean, ye dunno whit to do, dunno whit to say. Every cunt's
edgy, clockin each other, stampin the feet, rubbin the hands
together an coughin. Aye, ye know that awkward cough ye
do? Whistlin. Ye even try whistlin.
Aw, some cunt break the ice, for fuck sake.
Somebody starts the ball rollin.
Fuck it lads, come on, don't let him get to us. Come on, we'll
show the bastart. Hasn't a clue, the cunt. Office boy. Probably
had his dick skelped with the high heedyins for somethin an

havin a go at us for it. Aye, c'mon, forget it, it's just his way, man. His bark's worse than his bite. Does that with every cunt, it's nothin personal, c'mon to fuck.

Mad Dog just stans there. Says nothin. Doesn't need to. Mad Dog's got a glass head, y'can see right in. What's it like, eh? Inside his head it's like a fuckin Rolex with the cogs clickin away turnin the wheels. Aye, a finely tuned watch tick tick tickin away like a time bomb.
Tick tick tick tick tick. Clear as day. The mad mind at work.

Doesn't he start rantin.

Dirty useless bastart. Havin a go, havin a go at yer, man, eh?
Ah mean, who's fault is it the fuckin chips are manky?
What the fuck does he want ye to do, scrub the bastarts? Take each fuckin chip an scrub it? Ah mean, there's thousans of the little cunts. Take ye a fuckin month, man.
An the cheeky bastart's got the balls to say the jobs a bit rough too, cheeky cunt.
Fuckin out here in all sorts of weather, so we are, puttin down tar that's fuckin shite to start with an it's the middle of winter an yer dick's fallin off with the cold an the fuckin water's runnin down the crack of yer arse, an the cunt's got a cheek to say it's a bit rough.
A bit rough?
The cheeky bastart. What the fuck does he want, eh?
Big dirty rotten bastart needs taught a lesson. Needs fuckin knocked down a peg or ten.

Mad Dog's gone. The auld time-bomb's done too many ticks.
The fuse is fuckin lit, sssssssssssssssssssssssssssssssssssssssssssssssssssssssss
BANG.
The rantin n ravin machine's moved into his head an livin rent

free. Big guy's para'd up bad. Says the high heedyins are after
him.
Aye, the hierarchy. The faceless wonders. He says they've been
after him for years so they have, years. An they've sent Marcus,
Marcus golden boy, whizz kid, the man with the golden pen.
That's right, stroke of a pen an he can wipe ye out, that's what
he's all about, that's his job.
The dirty rotten fuckers. They're tryin to waste yer man. Tryin
to get him sacked. Fuckin sacked, man. Sacked. On the scrap
heap. Can't feed the wife an weans. The poor weans, starvin
to death cos of these bastarts. Aye, that's what they're up to.
No chance. No fuckin chance, man. Never. Never ever ever ever
ever.

Mad Dog's flipped his lid completely, lost the fuckin plot.
Listen, see that noise ye hear. That grindin E-sharp nails down
a blackboard screechin noise. D'ye know what that is?
That's the fuckin paranoia screamin out of Mad Dog. Screamin
like banshees in hell.
He's jumpin up an down an pointin. Pointin down the road
after Marcus. Gonni knock the fucker out. Give it the auld
upstairs downstairs, one two, one two. Bang bang bang bang.
Fold him like a tuppenny book.

Naw, naw, naw, ah can't, he goes. Can't. Get a grip, fuck.
That's what they're wantin. That's the very thing the cunts are
watchin for. They're fuckin watchin, lads, they're watchin.
Ah'm tellin yees, troops, they're watchin right now. Watchin
every move. Aye, hidin somewhere. In the back of a van
mibbee. The auld camcorder rollin. That's the plot, ah'm tellin
yees.
Just watch, just fuckin watch, the bold Marcus'll come up an
start givin it the lip, the auld heavy-duty provocation stuff.

Start pickin at us proddin at our minds with the finger, man,
stickin it in there an turnin it round an round, grindin away,
goadin, goadin, goadin. Watchin for the red mist to drop. He's
tryin to break us down, boys, tryin to make us snap. Snap.
Snap just like that. He's tryin to make me snap, troops, lose the
auld rag an give him the auld bang bang bang bang routine.
That's what he's up to, ah can see it now. Can see it clear as
day.

Bang bang bang bang
T I M B E R

down he goes like a condemned tower block an the next thing
ye know they'll come screamin out the back of a transit. Got
ye, ya bastart. Caught. Caught on Candid Camera. Ah'm tellin
yees, troops, they're watchin us.

Aw, big Mad Dog. Poor big Mad Dog. Gone. Gone with the
wind. Bubbly white grog foamin out his lips.
We're all just standin about.
Whit we gonni do, man? Whit?
Shop the cunt?
Na, couldn't. Pointless.
He's a Fourth Division player, Marcus. That's a fact by the way,
ah'm tellin ye. When it comes to the auld corruption games he
hasn't got a look in with these cunts at the Town Hall, man.
Just a boy. Just a novice. Just a fuckin bit-player. It would
probably get him Brownie points, shoppin him. All the fat cats
would be givin it pants-pissin frenzy, man. Pattin him on the
back tellin him, Well done, son. Good boy good boy, oh yes yes
yes, crush the small people.
Go a long way that young chap. Reminds me of me in my
young day. A real scoundrel, that boy.
Naw, that's shite that. Anyway that'd make us grassin bastarts.

Mad Dog hates grassin bastarts. Hates them.

That bastart Marcus. We'll sort him.

How but? How?

Enter Sid.
Take a look at him now, boy. The Silky Sid. What's he like, eh?
Campin it up, wigglin the walk, the high-pitched talk. That's
what happens, innit? Once they're out, they're out. Oh fuck
aye, man, let it all hang out. No more hidin an shammin it up,
naw, they just let it rip, start givin it the auld this-is-the-real-
me patter.

Does no work, Sid. Well, he's Mad Dog's mate, isn't he? Aye, he
just keeps the place tidy, makes the tea, goes to the shops.
Honest to fuck, that's all he does, ah'm tellin ye. The queeny
boy Sid's got it made. Life of Riley. Just struts about there
lookin pretty.
Pretty as punch. Check that ass in those jeans. Painted on. The
fuckers are painted on, so they are. Draws a few looks too.
Some of the troops have been caught havin a gander, a wee
quick squint. Always quick as fuck to play it down but, aye,
make a joke out it.

Haw, you ya big cunt, that's some arse, better arse on ye than
that wife of mine. No jokin.

Got to watch but. Take it easy, don't go over the score. Ah
mean, ye hear about it every day about cunts turnin over,
y'know? Jumpin the fence.
Aye, been straight as the horizon all their days. Married,
weans, granweans even. Then the next minute. Bang.
Bob's yer boyfriend an they're offski-pop down the road with
the lover boy givin it all this couldn't-help-myself patter, ah've

been stiflin these feelins since ma teens, so ah have, honest.
Aye, been fightin them all ma days, tryin to control the urge,
livin a lie, livin a lie all my life until one day ah saw this
gorgeous arse an
BAM
FIREWORKS.
Aye, that's how it all starts, man. Watch what yer doin.

Sid told Mad Dog about Marcus.
See him, he says, that cunt over there? He's bent.

Mad Dog looks at him. That look, ye know the one. Sarky, that
sarky look he gives ye an then rolls the eyeballs to the sky an
lets out a heavy sigh an drops the shoulders. Aye, he looks at
Sid like that.

Aw, him over there's bent, Mad Dog says, doin a Sid voice, all
soft an she-she. It's far too deep but. Aye, too deep. Ye can tell
it's not Sid a mile off.

Mad Dog shakes his head. Aw, tell us somethin fuckin new, he
goes. Fuck sake, what're ye on about? Get real you, ya cunt,
will ye, eh? Fuckin wise up.

No no sweetie, Sid says.

Aye, Sid calls Mad Dog sweetie an Mad Dog just stans there an
doesn't bat an eyelid. Naw, just smiles an shakes his head.
Ach, anyway. Fuck it. Wait till ye hear this bit.
Sid put's the big man in the picture. Tells him not that kinda
bent.
Naw, what he means is bent bent. Hoofter poofter type bent.
Aye, the same as Sid only different. Worse. Closet job. Married,
two weans, respectable pillar of the community.
But when darkness falls. Well, that closet door opens an the

bold Marcus is on the rampage. Prone to a taste of the auld pishy public toilets is our Marcus. Aye, a well-kent face among the bogs an public park boys.

Mad Dog stans there, mouth open, billiard-ball eyes, like a lottery winner watchin the screen an realisin the six numbers are his. Aye, they're all his but he can't believe it, man, he just can't believe his luck. Needs reassured.

Are ye sure, man, are ye, are ye sure, are ye fuckin sure yer sure?

Sid sticks his chest out, grogs on the deck an growls, The Pope's a Jungle Jim an King Billy's a Proddy an cows do big watery turds in the fields.

Aye, Sid does a Mad Dog. Not bad. Too high-pitched but.

Aw, Holy Jesus, man. Mad Dog looks at the sky. The heavens open an the sun sprays glittery sprinkles of gold across the sky. Mad Dog's got a plan. A crazy idea. He puts his arm round Sid. Makes him a promise. Mentions that wee deal. Remember the one in the canteen, ten quid for a stroke at the auld dick? Well Mad Dog makes him a promise.

Help me pull this one off, he says, an yer man here's poadjer's all yours. Do what ye like with it, stroke it chew it take big chunks out it with yer teeth. Pull this one off an it's on the house ma boy, on the fuckin house.

The two of them start huggin an laughin. Well, just-havin-a-bit-of-crack type huggin y'know? Just a joke.

Mad Dog gets the auld this-is-how-we're-gonna-play-it-head on.
This is what happens.

The Marcus man trundles up this day in the jeep.
He gets out an breezes over givin it the swagger that ye could
dry a washin on.

Up struts Silky Sid an starts chattin away like. Aye, he starts
chattin away heavy-duty style, man, really layin it on thick.

For fuck sake, talk about feelin awkward. The auld Marcus
Manley boy doesn't know where to look. The big cool dude
Jack the Lad hung like a fuckin donkey lady-killer Marcus
standin bummin to the Silky Sid. Doesn't know where to stick
his head, so he doesn't. Just wishes his arse could open up an
he could stick his head up it. Ye see, this is different. Ye're out
here in the open. Can't hide in the shadows now, boy.
Aw, this is his worst nightmare, so it is. Standin all alone talkin
to a plucked eyebrowed bum boy. An nowhere in the world
to hide.
It don't look good, bro. Does fuck-all for the street cred.

Fuck me, he's sweatin cold pish. He's been outed in front of
every cunt an their auntie.
He throws the bluff card an starts givin it idle chit-chat.
Daft stuff like, ye know?

Not a bad day, thought it was gonni rain, sort of shit.
Did ye see the soccer last night did ye?
How's the material?
Havin any problems with the traffic cops?

Aye, all that shit. Daft bastart's stumped, man, doesn't know
where to turn, wants to die, wants the fuckin sky to open up
an sook him in.
It gets worse too. Oh fuck aye, this is where it gets worse.

Up struts Mad Dog.

Aw, for fuck sake, not big Mad Dog, Marcus is sayin under his breath. Aw naw, aw naw, aw fuckin naw. The bold Marcus starts shittin rabbits. Mad Dog? The last cunt on earth he wants to see.

Mad Dog gives it, How's it goin, bro? his big beady eyes bouncin between Sid an Marcus.
You two cunts know each other?

Hey, check Marcus out now. What's he like, eh?
His sweaty arse is bleetin like a nuclear war siren. It fuckin is, the auld sphincter muscles are goin like that:

BLEET BLEET BLEET BLEET BLEET

Mad Dog stares hard down the barrels of his eyeballs, drillin them hard into the fucked-up mind of poor Marcus.

He puts his arm round Sid an says, Ma silky pal here could swear he knows you from somewhere but can't quite put the painted fingernail on it.

Sid rolls his tongue round his lips, sucks in hard an says, It's not so much the face that's familiar but the body, it's the body, ooooooh that firm muscular body, those tight buttocks, those firm meaty thighs, that hairy chest.

Knob throb. Marcus takes a knob throb. Swear it, man. Honest to fuck. Ye could see it.

That's it, Sid goes, that throbbin knob an bulldog balls. Held them in ma hans an stroked them with these dainty fingers. Where but, where? Aw, my God it's comin, it's all comin back but it's not so clear, no it all seems very hazy. Cloudy. Steamy. Yeeeeeeehaaaaaaaaaaaaaaaaaaaa steamy. Steamy steamy steam fuckin steamy. The steamroom, man.

The steamroom at the sauna where it's all hand jobs an blow
jobs an that mind-blowin ball-bustin arse-tinglin buzz of
fuckin an absolute stranger in the dark

ooooooooooohhhhhhhhhhhhhhhhhh.

Mad Dog frowns an sooks in hard. Looks like he's just watched
a striker miss a sitter.

Tut tut tut tut tut, he goes. Fuckin hell, man. Unprotected sex?
Unprotected gay sex? An in these AIDS-ridden times. My fuck,
man, dodgy dodgy dodgy.

Mad Dog starts tellin Marcus that he's really shocked an
stunned.

Aw, fuck aye, he says, shocked an stunned to say the least
Marcus, son. Thought you were a ladies' man too, honest to
fuck. Still, ye know what they say, don't knock it till you try it.
One man's fanny is another man's arsehole. Or somethin like
that. But you should be more careful. That lovely wee wife of
yours, ah mean, if she found out it would break her fuckin
heart.
An yer poor wee weans, the slaggin they'd get at school. Cruel
wee cunts, weans.
Probably do a runner, so she would. Her an the weans. Just
think of the fuckin shame, man. Poor wee wife an weans.
Ah mean, ah take it she doesn't know?

The Marcus fellow starts bubblin. Aye, ah swear, bubblin like a
baby. We're all standin there givin it, Aw, ya fuckin big pussy.
Who's the fuckin smart-arse now, eh? Big flash cunt shaggin all
the burds, ma arse. Been out there sookin dicks, ya fucker. Hey,
come on big macho-man, dry yer eyes. Yer number's up, ya
cunt. The game's a fuckin bogey.

Marcus starts pleadin like fuck with Mad Dog. Tells him to name his price. You name it, you can have it, he says. What do you want? Anythin, man, anythin at all, it's all yours, come on big guy ah'm fuckin pleadin, please please please. Aw, how much do ye want, eh? Couple of gran? More? Five? Ten? Just name it, name yer fuckin price.

Mad Dog smiles, shakes his head an tells him it's alright. It's alright Marco baby, stop fuckin whingin an dry yer eyes. The Mad Dog don't want yer money. What do you take me for? Sid lets out a squeal. A real high-pitched number an all, ah'm tellin ye. Aye, a real fuckin-just-put-a-ladder-in-ma-stockins style squeal. Eeeeeeeeyyyyaaaaaawwwwww, he went.

He can't believe it. The Sid boy can't believe it, man. He doesn't want money? Mad Dog doesn't want money? What the fuck's goin on? What's it all about, eh? Brought poor Marco baby out the closet for nothing.

Oooooooooooohhhh such a fuckin shame.

Naw, Mad Dog says, blowin out long smoke jets an starin at the sky rubbin his chin. No money, man. Just a small teensie weensie midge's-dick-size favour.

The look on Marcus's face says, Aye, anythin, any fuckin size favour you like.

Easy as pie, Mad Dog goes. Easy as a Coatbridge barmaid. This is it in a nutshell.

He starts givin the Marcus man a road-buildin lecture.

The big planin machine rips out one hundred mill, right? Yer good self comes along an dips his wick, if ye pardon the pun, an make sure it's deep enough. OK?

Along come us troops an lay sixty mill of base.
Along comes your good self an dips it for depth.
Along come the troopaderos again an lay forty mill of asphalt.
Right, so we've now got one hundred mill out. An one
hundred mill in. Magico. Championi. A guy called Robert's just
married yer mammy's sister. Right?

Poor Marcus. Aw, poor fuckin Marcus, man. Poor cunt's more
confused than ever. Standin there sweatin buckets an greetin
an snotterrin an doesn't know what's happenin to him an
what the fuck's all this road buildin shite an wishin Mad Dog
would just take the money an be done with it.
Poor Marcus wants his mammy.
Mad Dog pinches Marcus's cheek an puts his arm round him,
squeezin.

This is your job, ya big leather-joy-boy ye. Talk to the planer
driver. A wee word in his shell-like. Tell him just to rip out
eighty. Eighty mill. Aye.
The boy'll be delighted, man. Less work for him an it won't be
as sore on his machine an there'll be less shite to take away
which means he's loused earlier which means more time for
him to head down the boozer.
Magico. No questions asked an every fucker's happy as a coke-
head in Colombia.

Marcus nods. Been noddin non-stop, so he has. Noddin like
fuck. Aye, look at him. Noddin like a hangin monkey in the car
rear window. Ye know the type? The wee noddin monkey that
tummels its wulkies. That's Marcus for ye.

Bold he-man Marcus no more.
He shuffles away. What's the cunt like, eh? Check the fuckin
lip. The auld lip's goin like the fingers round a mouth organ.

Ye know the style? Ye know when they give it the wa wa wa wa bit? Aye, that. The Marcus boy's lips're goin like that.

Poor Sid, man. Poor auld Sid. Ah mean, he's been confused all his life, the poor cunt. Well ah'll tell ye this for fuck all, he's more confused now. Confused as a cult member, standin there with a what's-it-all-about look on his pretty little face.

What's the fuckin score, man, what's the Hampden Roar? All this sixty mill, eighty mill, a hundred mill shit. What the fuck?

Mad Dog looks at him. Gives him the look. Y'know the one? Gives him a are-ye-daft-for-fuck-sake-think-about-it look.

Right, let me spell it out to ye, watch ma fuckin lips, he goes.

The job's just eighty mill deep, right? Forty base, forty asphalt. Well, it had been measured for one hundred, right? Ye're with me so far, eh? So it's twenty mill shallower than they thought. That's twenty fuckin millimetres that doesn't need tarred. Got me? Which means, my old fruit, there's tar left over.
Doesn't sound much. Twenty mill. Naw, sounds fuck-all if ye say it fast. But just think about it. Use that pretty little pink think-tank God gave ye.
Twenty mill spread over thousans of metres. Thousans, man, ah mean, these fancy tar machines lay the auld black stuff round the clock, so they do. Ah'm tellin ye, man, they drop more tons of shit than a herd of elephants.
So like ah say, there's all this stuff left over. Hundreds of tons left over. Hundreds of tons of black shit lyin up at that quarry doin nothin, man, nothin. Just lyin there twiddlin its fuckin thumbs waitin to be picked up an spread in some poor cunt's driveway at extortionately low prices.

Silky Sid's still in the dark.

Still can't suss it, man, all this hundreds of tons of tar lyin up at
the quarry shit. So what, man, so fuckin what? What good's it
doin lyin up there?
Enter Stan the Man. Aye, Stan the Man. The Quarryman. The
gaffer on the weighbridge. Yer man Stan an Mad Dog go back
yonks. Fuckin donkeys. Honest to fuck, the cunts were stealin
motors when Mother Theresa was in the Brownies.
Bob's yer auntie. Stan an Mad Dog are in business.
All that tar lyin up there an yer man Stan in charge. Aw my
fuck, man, we're talkin tar on tap. Honest to Christ. Talk about
pennies from Heaven? Well listen, ah'm tellin ye it's fuckin
rainin blackstuff here. Pourin out the sky, so it is. Endless
asphalt. Enough tar to lay a driveway that goes ten times
round the fuckin universe an back.

Aw, man, that's when it all started. The singin. That stupit
fuckin song. How does it go?

> We are the Crazy Gang
> The Crazy Gang are we.

That was the start of it. The anthem. The Crazy Gang's anthem.
We even done the guitar noises, so we did. Aye, y'know the
wee bits that go

> deeet deaaaawww dee ree ree   dee dee deee dee
> deee deeee deaaaaawww   deee reeeeaawwww

We even done that.
So there we are all givin it pelters on the guitars when the
bold Sid pops up.

Hold it, he goes, standin there smilin an all soft n sexy.
Hey, big boy, what about our deal? Ye'know the one you
mentioned? Stroke it, lick it, bite it, chew it, hit myself over

the head with it till ah'm black an blue. Remember?

Mad Dog takes a run an launches a size ten steel toe-capped boot right up Sid's tight little shiter.

Oooooooooooooooooooh big boy, Sid says. I never knew you cared.

Chapter Twelve.
The Crazy Gang.

We needed bigger rakes an bigger wheelbarrows. Ah'm tellin ye, our own little private tar factory was rakin it in. Hey listen, we were gettin beggin letters from Donald Trump. Swear it. Get to fuck, ya beggin bastart.

An ah'll tell ye what else. We were gettin steamin drunk every night, man. Aye, blitzed out our nappers all the way to the bank. Easy street. We were on easy street. The auld Crazy Gang. Singin our song. Singin our anthem.

> We are the Crazy Gang
> The Crazy Gang are we.
> Big beer bellies
> An sweaty, smelly feet.

Aw, we were singin it, man. Day in day out. Singin our fuckin tonsils out.

Mad Dog's in jail. We're all guilty. Fifty quid a job we were gettin. No questions asked. No worries. No complaints. No regrets. Fifty sheets, man. Fuck ye. Right into the hipper. Mad Dog done all the dealin. Aye, ye want to have seen this. Wore the auld collar an tie, so he did. Round the doors he'd go, chappin away like fuck givin out leaflets.

> MD & Son. Asphalt Co.
> Road Surfacing.
> Driveways. Paving Slabs. Fencing. Drainage.
> Weeding. Seeding. Soiling.

No job too big no job too small. Crazy Gang done them all.

Ah'm tellin ye, by the way, we'd knock back nothin but
syphilis.
We were the heavy-duty bullshit brigade.

Ye want to have heard the auld Mad Dog filla givin it the
patter. He'd stand there all spruced up to the nines givin it, Oh
what a lovely piece of property you have here, sir. Ever think
how classy it would look with a lovely tarmac driveway?
Oh yes sir. The icing on the cake.

Aye, ye want to have heard the porkies he told cunts.

What we would do here, sir, is we'd start of by excavating all
this broken-up rubble. Then we would dig down a metre deep
an take away all the muck an clay an all this other mushy shit.

Aye, ye want to have heard the cunt sir this an sir that.
Brought a tear to the head of yer knob, so it did.

Yes, sir. That's what we'd do. Dig it out, take it away, put in a
good solid bedrock an two layers of sub-base followed by a
two-inch layer of fine hot-rolled asphalt. Polish that off with
some fine stone edgings an lovely beach pebbles round the
edges. Solid as the old Gibraltar Rock. Drive a tank battalion
up an down it all day, so you could. Last an absolute lifetime.
Lifetime guarantee. Embarrassingly low prices, sir. Find anywhere cheaper, we'll give you your money back.
Do back door patios too, sir. Fancy a pink an grey chessboard-
style patio? Just think, madam, no more up to yer knees in
muck when yer hangin out the auld washin. Make a great wee
play area for the kiddies. Lovely wee suntrap too, so it is. Just
imagine lovely hot summers lyin out here bronzin up.

Honest to fuck, man, cunts were queuin up givin us business.
Couldn't keep them goin, so we couldn't. Wasn't enough

hours in the day, not enough days in the week. Eight days a week, we needed. Aye, we needed an extra day.
That was another anthem we had.
The Bizness.
Mad Dog used to say that years ago. See if we landed a right cushy number, the auld Dog filla used to say, aw, fuck, man this is the bizness, the fuckin bizness, so it is, eight days a week, ah could do this, so ah could.

An then he'd start singin.

> Thisss izzz the bizzz–nesss
> Ah fuckin well luuvv it.

Aye, that's what he used to do. Used to put the words to all his own songs.

Fuck aye, times were good, so they were. Party-time round the clock. We had the auld swally-heads on every night.
This is the Bizness was gettin chanted good style.
Fuckin cruisin. Cruisin so we were.

Ah'm tellin ye the auld Crazy Gang were

> crooooooooooooooosin.

We chapped this cunt's door this day.
Aw, fuck me, man. We knew the face. Knew the face well.
Couldn't think of his name but.
He was famous, man. Aye, it was him off the telly. Aw, what the fuck's his name? Aw, Jeez, man. Still can't think. Big gangly guy with buck teeth. Glaikit-as-fuck lookin.

We're all standin there with the auld eyeballs poppin out our heads.
Ye want to have seen this house. Aye, big sandstone mansion

with two sports cars, a Merc an a jeep.
We stood an imagined the inside.

Picture it. Bet ye it's got a swimmin pool an a jacuzzi an a
snooker room. Bet ye it's got four-poster beds an mirrors on
the ceilin an a private cinema for showin all the worlds fuckin
kinkiest porn films.
Aye, an ah bet the cunt holds mad coke-snortin orgies every
night of the week, the lucky bastart. Aye, bet the fuckin
thing's got a bondage dungeon jam-packed with rampant
rubber-wearin shaggin machines.

See what ah mean. Mind what ah told ye earlier? The tarman's
imagination's wilder than a four-year-old-wean's.
Oh fuck aye, man. Inside the mind of a tarman. Spoooookeee.

Mad Dog hits him with the three-layers shit.
He starts noddin. Smilin. Lookin well impressed. Aye, check
him out, man, big rich an famous cunt off the telly just about
to get well an truly turned over by the Mad Dog.
Ah'll tell ye how. Ah'll tell how he's just about to get well an
truly taken to the cleaners.
Ye'd never in yer craziest fuckin fantasies imagine what the
big cunt goes an does next.
Know what he does? D'ye know what the big soft cunt goes
an does next, man? Believe this or believe this not. The big
cunt goes an pulls out the wallet. Aye, a fuckin wallet, man.
Big hefty crocodile-skin number it was too. Aye, honest. We're
all standin there with the tongues hangin down by our balls in
amazement as the big filla peels off note after note after note
an slips them into Mad Dog's big sweaty palm.

Aw, Jesus, man, Jesus.
Mad Dog shoots his muck all over the guy's doorstep an

thanks him like fuck an tells him he'll be back first thing in the morning to get started on his driveway.

Aye, that'll be shinin bright. Driveway? What fuckin driveway, ya big doss cunt ye. Get yerself to fuck.

Listen, see the minute ye get the money up front, the party's over. The ball's burst. The game's a fuckin bogey, ah'm tellin ye, by the way, a pure big green slimy bogey.

But it turned out to be a bastart, so it did. A pure bastart. We couldn't get this famous cunt's name. Day in day out we'd sit there an drag the auld grey matter through the mincer.

Aw, what the fuck's his name now? These things haunt ye. Torment yer happiness. Bastart. The fuckin name flashes on yer mind for a billionth of a second.

Bang.   Flash.

Gone.

Just like that. Tearin at the tendons of yer brain muscles. Yer brain would be workin like a Taiwan sweat shop puttin together the pieces. An sometimes ye'd nearly get it too. Ye'd be like, Aw, it's nearly there, it's nearly there, an just as yer auld napper's about to press the Send button an spout it out.

Pop.

It's gone, man, it's fuckin well gone an it's drivin you so fuckin mad yer gonni jump up an down an start pullin yer baw hair out by the hanful an yer gonni chew off all yer fingers an gouge yer fuckin eyeballs out with boilin hot rusty garden shears.

Aaaaaaaaaarrrgggghhhhhhhh
        fuck fuck fuck fuck fuck fuck fuck fuck fuck fuck fuck.

Put it out yer mind, ye tell yerself. But ye can't, can ye? Naw, ye can't. Can ye fuck. It haunts ye, it fuckin well haunts the livin daylights out yer arse.

Day an night, man, day an night scrapin at yer brainbox like a fork down a blackboard. It talks to ye so it does, aye, that big fuckin face talks to ye. Ye can hear it.

Ah'm here, it's goin, ah'm here. It's me it's me it's me, the daft-lookin cunt off the telly with the long face an buck teeth.
It flashes on yer mindscreen all the time, man.
His face. His face. Aw, we just keep seein his face, an he's smilin, the dirty rotten fucker's always smilin.

The letters of his name rumble up yer throat an dance along yer tongue, man. Right on the tip of yer tongue they sit, comin together formin into words. Two words, man, that's all yer wantin, the two words. His name, aw, his name, it's nearly there, it's so near you can taste it, chew it, nearly tie yer jaw, in knots tryin to spit it out, fuckin spit it out ya bastart.
What's his name, man, what the fuck's his name?

Bang. Just like that. One day he just showed up. Aye, he just showed up, right out the blue. The glaikit glum cunt.
Fuckin profit of doom. There he was, man, on the telly an he's goin, Aw, life's just terrible. Terrible. Ah just found out my son's a jobby-jabber. An ma daughter, ma wee lovely daughter. She tells me she's expectin twins.
An the wife. The wife's just came out an told me straight, doesn't love me any more. Says she's been unfaithful. Twice. Aye. Been unfaithful twice. Once with the guy next door. An once with the Boys Brigade. Aw, terrible. Terrible, life's terrible.
An then just to top it all, as if life didn't stink enough, ah gave this big hairy guy two gran up front to tar ma driveway an ah've never seen him since.

Lucky White Heather.
Lucky White Heather.

Aye, that's who it was. The big guy off the telly. The big Lucky White Heather man.
What about Mad Dog but? Two gran up front. Kept that quiet, the big fly bastart.

Lucky White Heather right enough, man. Ye know what it's like. It only takes one to start the ball rollin. Aye, all it takes is one celebrity to bring it to light an every cunt an their auntie decides to get in on the act.

Honest to fuck, nobody had bothered their arse up until then. Not a fuckin cheep from no cunt. But see as soon as the big celebrity draws attention to it. Fuck ye, man, Joe Public are onto it like a horny dog gettin a whiff of a bitch's arse.
Talk about openin a can of worms? We're talkin a forty-five gallon drum full of forty-foot pythons here.
Cunts started comin out the woodwork ten-a-penny, man. Aye, layin it on thicker than a tarman at the doctor's lookin for a sick note. Ye want to have heard the shit that was goin about. Bogus workmen. Cowboys. Heartless scum.
Joe Public got story-toppin.

STORY 1
This dude's greetin about his driveway.
Aw, ma driveway, ma driveway. Check the fuckin mess. Three layers of tar, they told me. Aye, three layers they said an they gave me all this fancy patter about it bein solid as a rock an that ah would be able to drive fuckin tanks up it. Aye, right. Two days, two fuckin days, an guess what happened? Ah drive ma car on it an, whooooompf, down it goes like a white heavyweight. Fuckin plop, vanished, disappeared. The wheels

just disappeared, so they did. Ah couldn't get the fuckin doors open.

STORY 2
Tell ye a better one than that, the next cunt says. Ah paid the cunts thousans so ah did, an they gave me all the pish talk about bedrock, sub-base, puttin in new drainage, renewin all the pipes to make sure the ground won't hold any water. Naw, no chance of water lyin there, no way sirree. Yer auld driveway'll stay dry as a nun's nan-pot, so it will.
Aye. Right.
Fuckin woke up the next day, man, thought ah was still dreamin. Thought ah was out in fuckin Africa on safari. All ah see is big murky swamps, man, aye, right where my good driveway was the night before. A big fuckin murky swamp bubblin away like a pot of fuckin stew. Ah'm tellin ye, big fuckin slabberry-jawed crocodiles jumpin out it an takin big chunks out yer arse.

STORY 3
Tell ye a better one than that. Ah can top that one no bother. That's fuck-all compared to what the bastarts done to me.
Aye, they said they'd give it the usual three layers treatment an then soak it in this special weedkiller that destroys weeds for ever. Aye, gave me all this bullshit about it bein an acid formula that worked like an atomic bomb scorchin its way right down to the roots contaminatin the ground an burnin them into fuckin powder so that any kinda young up-an-comin weeds that came along an fancied settlin down an makin it their territory would be onto a fuckin darky. They said the auld ground would be like the earth after the H-bomb.
An then on top of that, to make extra certain, these sheets of specially-designed extra-strong polythene would be put down

just in case of that hundred million to one chance that one tiny little survivor weed might drag its badly scorched body to the surface.

Oh yes, sir, they said, got to be extra sure. Can never be too careful, never take chances.

Next day ah thought ah was fuckin seein things. Thought the auld eyes had gone colour-blind.

Black to green. Aye, ma fuckin driveway had gone from black to green over-night, so it had.

A lovely blacktop driveway? Was it fuck, man.

Fuckin greentop. A lovely greentop driveway.

No weeds?

Bastartin thing looked like a giant snooker table. Didn't know whether to drive on it or set the fuckin balls up for a few frames.

Cowboys. Fuckin cowboys.

We shit ourselves at this next bit. Fuckin shit runnin like molten lava down our legs. This cunt came on the telly an said he had our names. Aye. Told the Polis he had our names.

Ye want to know their names? he said. Wait an ah'll tell yees their fuckin names.

Buffalo Bill
Wyatt Earp
an Wild Bill Hickock.

Aye, good one, auld yin. Good one.

Chapter Thirteen.
The bad Good Friday.

It was all startin to do Mad Dog's nut in.

Aw, for fuck sake, this would do yer arse in, so it would. All this cash, man, it causes ye to drink like fuck, he used to say. Mad Dog was drinkin like fuck more than ever.
It ended up it did do his arse in. Done his arse in for real, so it did. It happened on Good Friday. Aye, definitely Good Friday.

What the fuck's good about it? he'd say. Had all these wee mad sayins, Mad Dog.

A fast day? he'd go. Good Friday, a fast day? Not fuckin fast enough, man, ah'm tellin yees.

Aye, it was funny the way he used to say it.
Well, every cunt would laugh, put it that way.
Anyway, why am ah so sure it was Good Friday?
Wait an ah'll tell ye.

We were in the boozer an it was only about ten o'clock when the bold Mad Dog starts checkin the clock. He's givin it this fuck-me-is-that-the-time-aw-look-at-the-time-fuckin-time-just-flies-when-yer-enjoyin-yerself-aw-fuckin-time-just-goes-like-that patter.
Mad Dog was on a final warnin, ye see. His last chance, man. Last chance saloon.

Had to get down the road. She was goin haywire. Blowin his ear drums out the top of his head with all this patter about how her an the weans never see him. Never seen him sober.

Aye, the weans dunno what their auld filla looks like. Ah'm tellin ye, the poor weans dunno they've got a Da. Better be straight home, ya cunt, she's goin.

She made him promise. Made him promise her an promise the weans. Straight down the road. Honest to fuck, gonni play the white, man. Holiday weekend an all that, gonni be good, spend some time with the weans, take them to the pictures, take them to the football, buy them sweeties, buy them toys, buy them any fuckin thing they want. Aye, all that shit.

Her words were ringin in his ears like a jack-hammer bouncin off concrete.

Ah mean it, ah fuckin well mean it, ya big cunt, ya big selfish bastart ye, ye better be down this road. Ye better, ya bastart. Last chance, big boy. Let those weans down this time, an we're offski.

Aye, all week he's been listenin to it.
So, as ye can imagine, the big boy's pissed off big time. He's got to go, man. Got to go. Got to head for the hills. One cunt of a mood. He doesn't want to leave, so he doesn't. Naw.

He's got to but. Got to get down that road. Home to her an the weans. Aye, that's right, her an the weans.
C'mon you, fair's fair, ya big bastart. Play the white, man, he can hear her voice tellin him right now.

But ye see the problem is, when yer full of the auld swally the mind takes on a voice of its own.
Aye, ye know what it's like. That wee voice.
Ye hear it goin, Ah fuck it, what's the hurry? Life's too short, innit? Chill out. Relax. Fuck sake, ye work all week, don't ye? Knockin yer pan in day in day out, fuckin head down arse up

an all yer lookin for at the end of the week is a couple of beers. Aye, just a couple of jugs, man, stan at the bar an relax, unwind, have a blether with the troops. Where the fuck's the harm in that, eh? C'mon, ah mean it's Friday, innit? It's pay day. Double dunt too, know what ah mean? Two weeks' wages an every cunt's a millionaire. Aye, millionaires all round, every fucker's got the holiday-head on an the auld drink's flowin like the Zambezi in a monsoon. C'mon, relax, unwind, take it easy. The auld crack's good. Fuck sake, where would we be if we couldn't have a laugh, eh? Aye, a man's got to have a laugh. Ah mean, what harm are ye doin, eh? Ah mean, ye fuckin well deserve it. Ye deserve it, that's a fact. The shitty jokes are flyin like pink elephants in a detox clinic. An this is the time to tell them too. Aye, y'know the ones that are a bit corny, an when ye tell them no fucker laughs? Well this is it, innit? Let them rip now, bro, cos everybody's wearin happy-heads an nobody gives a fuck about tomorrow cos life is just one big fuckin scream.

Mad Dog just wants to sit. Aye. The big filla's got the feelgood head on. He's got that feelin, man. Ye know what ah'm talkin about? That feelin when yer in no-man's lan, a sort of twilight zone where yer not drunk an yer not sober an ye wish ye could just sit there an soak in it forever.
Aye, Mad Dog wants to sit for ever an ever.

But he can't, can he?

Naw, can he fuck. Naw, cos he's got to go down the road. Aye, down the road, cos he fuckin promised, didn't he? Didn't he? Aye, he promised her, promised the weans.

She's gonni leave, man. Her an the weans are leavin.
Straight down the road, or they're off. Her an the weans are

off, man. Offski-pop. Swear to fuck, by the way, ah'll never forget Mad Dog's face that night. Trippin him, so it was. Aye, his face was away down there somewhere. The big filla's baw hairs were ticklin his chin, ah'm tellin ye. Sittin there like a Death Row con waitin to walk that walk. Ye know what ah mean? That two-mile walk towards the door. Here we come folks. Make way. Make way for fuck sake. Dead man walkin.

It ain't easy. Is it fuck.
Ye know what it's like too, don't ye?
An d'ye know the worst thing about it? Ye've got to listen to every cunt. The troops. Aye, all the troops are slaggin ye to fuck an whistlin at ye goin out the door.

They're all shoutin, Henpecked! Henpecked! Are you a man or a mouse? Eh? Eh? A man or a mouse? Squeak squeak squeak.

Aw, it's a bastart, a pure bastart.

So Mad Dog stoats out the door hatin the whole wide world an every fucker in it.
He starts staggerin down the hill shoutin at every cunt an any cunt. Shoutin at motors. Mad Dog hates motors. Fuckin pricks, he's shoutin. Shouldn't be on the fuckin roads. It's not safe to cross the fuckin street. Bastarts.

He just stoats right across the road.
Motors brakin, tyres schreeeechin, cunts swervin at the last minute an whizzin past his arse just missin him an no more. There's lights flashin an horns blarin.
Off the road, ya fuckin lunatic, cunts are shoutin.

Mad Dog screams at the sky, wavin the fists in the air an swingin the boot at motors. Bastarts, he shouts. Fuckin kills yees all, ya bastarts.

He puts the head down. Need to get home, man, need to get over the frog an toad, he's thinking.
He pulls the jacket shut. Turns the collar up.
A light wind's blowin thin rain on his face. Ye'll know the kind? Leaves ye soaked to fuck an ye don't hardly even notice it sprayin yer skin.

Damp mist's dancin across the street goin fuzzy round the edges of street lamps an car lights, leavin a greasy sheen on passin faces.

There's this right bad smell. It's comin from the shit factory under the bridge. Three young fuckers slitherin up the bankin. Crocs out a swamp. Three sets of bad eyes starin. Past carin. Stop at nothin, man. No respect.
They spy the drunk man stoatin down the hill three sheets to the wind. Just been paid an been to the boozer. The auld docket in the pocket ready for pickin.
No luck, man. Wrong place, wrong time.

Mad Dog walks like Quasimodo, so he does, the back hunched up an the head buried inside the jacket. Walks lopsided. Aye, walks like that when he's pished, man. Walks like one leg's shorter than the other. Remember the village idiot in *Ryan's Daughter*? Aye, him. Walks like him.
Easy target, eh?

Fuck ye, man. A dull thud. Mad Dog feels a dull thud right bang smack on the middle of the forehead. Beauty, so it was.
Right between the fuckin eyes.
Jeezaz fuck, what was that?
Somethin blunt.
A boulder? Baseball bat? Hammer? Take yer pick.
The big guy's not sure. Can't tell. Just feels this meaty squelch

an this fuckin horrible ball-burstin ringin in his ears.

He looks up at the sky an sees a billion sparklin street lamps
like electric orange dots bouncin across the blackness.
The young team stan there. Watchin. Waitin. Waitin on Mad
Dog goin down.
No way José. Not gonni happen. Mad Dog never goes down.
Never.
Red sticky warmth starts runnin past his eyes. It runs like hot
snot down his nose into his mouth touchin his tongue.
He tastes it. Blood.
Aw, the taste, man, the taste. Mad Dog loves that taste.
Adrenalin starts whooshin through his veins an his heart beats
like heavy rock, sendin electric shivers up his spine. He stans up
straight, expandin his chest. He grows six inches taller, six
inches wider. He stares like the Devil. His cold icy eyes freeze
over. Filthy rotten fuck-pigs, he snarls.
Show-time.
Let's do it.
He leaps through the air crashin the skull on a nose an starts
swingin the big paws, givin it the Mad Dog special. Bang bang
bang bang, two upstairs two downstairs. The guy folds like a
tuppenny book, so he does, an crumples onto the deck. He's
totally out it, man. Fuckin sparkles. Mad Dog locks his fingers
round the next cunt's neck like a pit bull's jaws an starts
squeezin hard.The guy goes limp an makes this weird noise. It's
kinda hard to describe. Y'know the noise cunts make when
they drink somethin an it goes down the wrong way? Aye,
that. Sounds somethin like that.

He's got this other fucker's hair. Big hanful of gelled-up hair.
Mad Dog's puttin his greasy head through the railins. Won't go
through at first, man. Too tight. Too tight a space. It's only

about four or five inches.
But Mad Dog never gives in, so he doesn't. Naw, he keeps
bangin an bangin makin the space go wider n wider as he
pushes the cunt's head through.

Aye, ye'll go through ya bastart, ye'll go through, he goes.

Aw, the noises, man. Horrible gut-churnin, flesh-tearin, teeth-
crunchin, eyes-gougin noises. Fuckin hauntin, so they were.
All these high-pitched howls like a hyena bein gang banged to
death by a bunch of horny gorillas.
It all happened quicker than ah can tell it. Much quicker. Can't
really tell it all. All the finer detail bits. Naw, just telling ye the
main story. The story ah've heard so often. Heard it so often,
man. A million times.

It's Mad Dog's party-piece. His story-topper. Any time there's
punch-up stories gettin told, Mad Dog throws this one in. Tells
it all the time, man. Tells it real good too. Tells it from the
heart, goes through all the actions, grabbin yer throat an yer
hair an jumpin up an down, headerin half an inch from the tip
of yer nose. Ah'm tellin, ye by the way, steer well clear when
he's tellin it, man.

Anyway, the three young team are lyin there moanin an
groanin, all bloody an booted to fuck.
One cunt scrambles to his feet an stoats away, bouncin off
walls an fences. Fucks off up the road sharpish leavin his mates
lyin there. Aye, fucks off an leaves the auld partners in crime
lyin there dyin like dogs in the street.
Honest to fuck, ye want to have seen this. Two heads smashed
faceless. One cunt's face is pressed right through the tar starin
into hell an the other fucker's head's stuck through the railins
with his fat spotty arse stuck in the air smilin at the stars.

D'ye know what Mad Dog went an done next? He went an pulled the guy's keks down an left his arse hangin open for some cunt to come along an park their bike.

That'll teach yees, he goes. Fuckin mess with the man. The main man. Numo Uno. Aye, not so fuckin smart now. Not so fuckin tough after all. Fuckin hard men? Wise guys? Now look at yees, look at yees. Fancy clobber, fancy hairdo. Not so pretty now. Naw, naw, lyin there stewin in yer blood an soakin in yer pish. Fuckin fuck-pigs.

All's quiet. No more jungle sounds. No more screamin kickin boakin choakin noises. Naw, just the sound of car tyres slushin on wet tar. Slowin down, havin a wee gander an then speedin away leavin nothin but tail lights fadin. Round here nobody stops. Never. Would you?

Mad Dog lums up. Got to get home, man. Need to get over the road. He puts the head down an starts walkin. Not far now, eh? Just over the hill an through the lane.
It takes all night but he gets there at last. He turns into his gate an looks up.

Bastart. Fuck ye fuck ye fuck ye fuck ye. Bastart.

The place is blacked out, innit? Total darkness.
She's offski. She's fucked off. Her an the weans. Ah mean, she'd warned him. Told him. She'd told him straight. Had enough. Had it up to here. Sick to death with all the drinkin an fightin. Had a fuckin bellyful of false promises an fucked-up excuses. Heard them all. Takin no more. Finito.

Fuckin bastart, man. Mad Dog's ragin. Went an left the pub early for nothin. Bastart. Fuck her. Mad Dog's had enough. He can't be bothered any more. He's feelin dead drowsy. It

must've been that wee bump on the head he got like,
ye'know? Aye, Mad Dog's feelin a bit queasy. Needs to lie
down, so he does. Lie down an crash the head.

Cunt, man. Fuckin cunt. No key. Mad Dog's lost the key.
Aw, ya bastart ye, fuckin bastart. Not again. Fuck.

We used to kid him on all the time, so we did. Haw, ya big
cunt, we'd shout, ye want to tie that fuckin thing round
yer neck so ye do, yer in the *Guinness Book of Records* for
losin keys.

Ah well, he thinks, fuck-all else for it. Time to put the auld size
tens through the door. Aye, piece ah cake to Mad Dog. The big
filla's the undisputed puttin-the-boot-through-doors-champion-
of-the-world.
Wait a wee minute but. Hold it. He takes a wee brainwave. He
remembers the auld kitchen window's a bit dodgy. Aye, the
latch at the top's loose. Been like that for years, so it has.
Always been meanin to fix it. That's the game, man. Mad Dog's
got it all sussed. He'll just stick the auld arm in, pull it up, an
squeeze through.
Easy peezy, man. Doddle.
He heads round the back. He clambers up on the wheely bin
an gives the window a wee push.
Fuckin cunt, man, it's stiffer than Frank Bruno.
He pushes a wee bit harder. Wee bit more. Wee bit more. Bit
more yet, nearly there, can hear it creakin, ready to give.

Next thing all ye hear's Crrrraaaaaaaaaaccccccckkkk, the whole
fuckin panel crashes an the auld wheely bin starts rollin.
Mad Dog birls through the air like a bovver-booted ballerina
an crashes arse-first through the space where there used to be
a kitchen window.

He smashes down on the sink, slides along the work top an drops like a turd out a cow's arse an lands in a heap on the deck. A million glass splinters go everywhere.
Mad Dog can't stop laughin. Hysterical. Aye, that's what he does by the way. Finds these kinda things a riot.
Why? You tell me.
So there he is, man, rollin about in the glass laughin like pure fuck. Well, as ye do, eh?
Used to piss hisself laughin, Mad Dog. Seriously. Used to laugh that much he'd piss his pants.
Mad Dog was a pisser. Did ah never tell ye that? Aw fuck aye, man. The big guy's the founder member of the auld splungers club.

So anyway, he puts his han under his arse an thinks he's done it again.

Ya bastart, he goes. Fuckin done it again. Aw, fuck.

But then he checks the auld han an notices it's all red.
Aye, pure crimson so it was. There was all this oily lumpy stuff like raw, liver spewin out yer man's shit box.
An the thing is, yer man's standin there that blitzed out his fuckin head that he can't work out what's goin on. Where the fuck's all the blood comin from?
Ye know what it's like when yer pished, man.
Ye can't feel fuck-all.

He stans up n drops the keks an moonies at the mirror.
Fuck me, he goes, whit the fuck?
There's this big slither of glass the size of a dinner plate wedged right across his shiter. Aye, right across his cheeks, man. Splittin his big arse into four quarters. Fuck sake, it's stingin like a billion bees. He's got to get it out so he has, it's

fuckin killin him. Aw, the pain, man. Pain in the arse.
Mad Dog's arse is sorer than a butt-fucked boy scout.

He bends right over an grabs the edges of the glass. He grits
his teeth an tightens his eyes.
Aw, for fuck sake, what's he like? The poor big cunt's sittin
there with a face like Charlie Chan wankin, an this big slice of
double glazin hangin out his arse.

He pulls.

Whoooooooooooooooooooooooooooshh.

Awwww ya fuckin beauty, man, what a relief.
Mad Dog feels his head goin light an all the blood whirlin
through his body like water whooshin up a gulley motor tube.
Aye, it feels like white-water rapids rushin right out his arse.
The fuckin rush, man, the rush.
Feels like the first two seconds of the auld vinegar stroke.
Some sensation.

So anyway, after all that the auld Mad Dog filla's fucked, man.
Shattered.
He's got to get the head down, got to get some bo-peep. Can't
keep the auld peepers open any longer, man. Fuckin fifty-
sixers hangin from the eye-lids. Spaced-out to fuck, so he is.

Weightless,
        floatin
              lighter
                     lighter

inside his head goes white.

                                  Out.

The next mornin the auld grapevine's hummin. Down here
word travels fast. Mad Dog's wife's heard the news.
She's heard there was a muggin last night under the bridge.
Three young team fuckin wasted some cunt. Heard it was
Mad Dog.

She heads round the road fearin the worst. Soon as she opens
the front door it smacks her right in the mush. The smell. The
usual. The smell of pish booze an stale farts. She turns her
head away. Her eyes go watery an she's ready to boak.
Then she sees the blood. She starts to shake.
There's blood smeared across the lobby wall an there's big
blobs of it all over the livin room door. The handle's caked.
She opens the door slow.
Keeks her head round.

Awwwwwwwwwwwww Holy Jeeeezaaaz.

She schreeeches like a set of dodgy brakes.

There it was, man. Lyin behind the door saturated in blood.
Every woman's worst nightmare. A sight no woman should
ever have to see. A sight she'll never forget. A picture that'll
tattoo itself in her mind forever.

Aye, there it was, man.
Her suite.
Her bran new three-piece suite. Ruined. Fuckin ruined.
She goes hysterical an starts howlin.

Aw, the dirty lousy bastart, she goes. Look at it. Look at it. Aw,
look at the state of ma lovely fuckin suite. Ruined. Fuckinwell
ruined. Aw, an look at ma good carpet an look at ma nice
curtains. Aw, the fuckin mess. Fuckin blood too, dried-in blood,
fuckin worst thing in the world. They're ruined. The big filthy

bastart, ah'll kill him, so ah will. Fuckin kill him.

Just at that his wee maw walks in. Aye, Mad Dog's maw's heard the word. See what ah mean, man? Loud tom-toms. Her face goes like the wife's. She stans there rooted to the spot. She can't believe it, man, so she can't. Can't believe her eyes. The mess. The blood. The place is like a fuckin butcher's shop.

Aw, Holy Mother ah God, she goes, ma laddie, ma wee laddie, what's happened to him, where is he?

They follow the blood. It starts in the kitchen, snakin its way across the sink, washin machine, fridge, an then slitherin out into the livin room an coilin into a big dirty turd-like stain on the couch.

Aw, the couch, the wife's sayin to herself. Aw, ma fuckin good couch.

Out in the lobby there's big red paw marks all over the radiator an there's size ten blood prints walkin right up the stair carpet.
Wee Maw an the wife follow the prints.

Aw ma laddie, the wee maw's goin, blessin herself an prayin to the Holy Mary on the wall. Aw ma laddie, ma poor wee boy. Please God Almighty, make him be alright.

Her. The wife. Ye want to hear her. Just can't get over it, man. No way. Her suite, her fuckin good three-piece suite.

Aw, in the name a fuck. Just got it too, just got it on the fuckin never never. Aye, two fuckin grands worth. Just started payin it an all, aye. One fuckin payment an it's ruined. Ruined. Aw, to fuck.

The footprints go round the corner into her an Mad Dog's
bedroom.
What's that? What's that noise? There's this light trundlin
noise. Wee footsteps comin up the stairs.
It's the wee filla. Wee JD. Wee Junior Dog.
It's pure fuckin mad panic stations now, innit? They've got to
keep him out.

Don't come up the stairs, they start shoutin. Naw, naw, naw,
stay where ye are, don't go in there, son. Naw, stay out.

They try to grab him.
No chance. Wee man's too fast. He just goes an shimmies
to the side an jukes in between them an barges through
the door.
He stops in his tracks.
His face turns whiter than a junky on bad gear.

Honest to fuck, the wee cunt could've changed his name to
Caspar, standin there with his eyes an mouth hangin open like
torn pockets.

So there he is. Standin there like he's just walked in on the
auld Santa filla.

He lets out this almighty roar.

The maw an the wife are out in the lobby huggin each other
tight. Eyes shut, can't look, can't bear to look, man.

The wee maw falls to her knees an starts givin it, Oh my God in
Heaven, aw, son, aw, son, aw, we're sorry son, poor fuckin
laddie, aw, my God aw, Holy Mary Mother of God.

Next thing wee JD shouts, Maw, Maw, Granny, c'mere, c'mere
an see this.

The two women tiptoe in dead slow an keek round the door.
An there it was, man. There it was.

The bold Mad Dog filla lyin there face down with the big bare
arse stickin up in the air.
Aye, this big bare arse with its usual slit down the way.
An this other big bloody slit runnin across it.

Look Maw, look, Junior Dog shouts. Look what's lyin on top of
your bed.
A big fuckin gigantic hot cross bun.

Aye, that's how ah can remember it was Good Friday.

Chapter Fourteen.
Nancy's last grunt.

Mad Dog was crackin up, man. Crackin up completely.
Goin mental so he was. Doo-lally. Sayin crazy things too.
Fuckin weird. Things ye wouldn't expect, man. Never. Naw, not
from Mad Dog.

Aye, sayin things like, Ye've got to watch yerself, man, ye've
got to watch this young team, ah'm tellin ye, fuckin crazy
bastarts, so they are. They're feart of no cunt. Got to watch
them, man, ye never know, never know what's in their fuckin
pockets.

Strange. Strange talk for Mad Dog.

He was missin her. Mad Dog was missin her. The wife. She.
Her an the weans done a runner. Fucked off for good after
that carry-on with the hot cross bun.

Fuck it, she said. Took a fast black.
No more shit. Had it up to here, so she had. Offski, man.

Mad Dog would sit there greetin about his wee house. Aw,
look at the wee cat n mouse. Shit-hole. A pure fuckin shithole.
Once had it nice too. Aye, had it like a palace. All nice an lady-
like. So fancy an chic. Way back when? Dunno. The good old
days. The good old days. Aye, in the beginnin. Everythin was
so sweet in the beginnin. All lovey dovey. Mad Dog even used
to hand over all the wages. The works, man, the whole fuckin
dockit. Here ye are darling, it's all yours.
Aye, in the tar game ye get to hear all sorts of weird an wonderful stories. Ye get to hear all the crack. Ye know what it's

like when yer standin in the boozer an ye get listenin? Listenin to all the stories cunts tell. Stories stories stories stories.

There was this story about some guy spoilin his wife rotten, ye know? Helpin her with the housework, goin shoppin, takin her out for meals.
Givin her all the wages even.
So what does she do?
Goes an takes the poor cunt for granted. Ah mean, he's just a fuckin sap. A borin dick-head. The woman wants more excitement.
Every woman wants excitement.
So she fucks off, man. Fucks off with her boss or his best mate that was best man at the weddin or some waiter that she met when her an her pals went on holiday. Aye, she got goin on holiday herself cos the doss cunt trusted her.
Or even worse still, man, she fucks off with another woman. Aw, for fuck sake imagine it, eh. Ah mean, it's alright fantasisin, innit? Ye know what ah'm sayin? Two burds getting it on an all that. But fuck me, imagine it happenin to YOU. The shame. Can ye imagine the fuckin shame?
Ah'm tellin ye, man, got to watch those burds. Fuck off an leave ye if ye treat them nice, so they will. Aye, take ye for granted, man.
Ah'm tellin ye by the way, got to fuckin watch them. Treat them mean an keep them keen. Aye, that's the sort of patter ye hear in boozers all the time, innit?
So anyway, Mad Dog heard that story one day.

Fuck me, he starts thinkin. Better start watchin, man. Givin her too much dosh. Decides to start takin a wee cut for himself. Five, mibbee ten per cent. Aye, fuck it, he says. Every other cunt's doin it. Ah mean, ye know what they say, no point in givin it to the wife if ye need it yerself.

Is that alright darlin? he asks. Alright if ah take a wee bit extra pocket money?

Naw, is it fuck, she says. Alright fuckin not. Han it over. The lot. Han the lot over now.

Fuck you bitch. Take it or leave it.

After that she never saw another dockit in her life. Never. She just got what Mad Dog gave her. An ah'll tell ye what else, she got less an less as time went by.
Aye, that's how it started, man. Honest.
That's how it all started.

It went from bad to worse for the big man.
Mad Dog started spending more an more time at Nancy's.
Never out the place, so he wasn't. Mornin noon an night. Ye want to have heard the fuckin slaggins he used to take.

Every cunt was goin, When's the weddin, big man, aye, when's the invites goin out? Just think, big guy, you an Nancy'll soon be takin a wee jaunt round Asda. Aw, what a lovely couple. Lovely babies yees'll make.

Mad Dog would laugh a wee bit an go, Fuck yees, ya cunts.

But see what ah was sayin about it goin from bad to worse. Well, then it went from worse to fuckin downright diabolical. D'ye know what happened by the way. Aw, ye'll never believe it. Nancy went an fuckin died. Aye, honest to fuck, by the way. Wait an ah'll tell ye.
It was just a normal run-of-the-mill night, so it was. We were all up the boozer well bevvied an we decided to get a cargo an hit Nancy's.

Mad Dog found her. Mad Dog found her dead.

Aw, poor Nancy, he started screamin. She's dead she's dead, aw my fuck, she's fuckin stone dead.

Those screams, man. Never forget them. Tattooed in ma mind for ever, so they are. Aye, right in there, man. Right into the auld mind-piece.

Thought it was a nightmare. Dreamin of screamin. Screamin.
Aw, those fuckin screams, man.
Who's were they? The screams? Dunno, man. Dunno.

Nightmare? Reality? Take yer pick.
All the fuckin same, man. All the one thing.

Poor Nancy. Never forget it. Lyin over there. Aye, over there in the corner. Aw, it was fuckin real alright. Can still feel it, so ah can. Feel it like it's happinin right now, bro.
Nancy was colder than December. Rock-hard.
Mad Dog hit her a slap.

Nancy Nancy Nancy. Wake up doll!

Aye, he called her doll. Mad Dog called her doll.
Wee slip of the tongue, big guy, eh?

But there was nothin, man. Not a fuckin thing. Her icy eyes just rolled over an lay half open, half shut.
Ah mean, don't get me wrong, we didn't think there was anythin out the ordinary there. She always done that. Swear to fuck by the way, the auld Nancy used to sleep with her eyes half-an-half. Fuckin spooky, so it was.
But anyway, we touch her, an Jesus she's cold. Blue with the cold. Aye, Nancy starts turnin blue. Her tongue an all. This big blue tongue slides out her mouth like a turtle's head keekin

out its shell on a new mornin.
An then we notice somethin in her mouth.
What the fuck's that in her mouth, man? What?
D'ye know what it was, by the way? A fuckin boak ball. Aye, a
boak ball the size of a half brick wedged in her throat.
Wedged tight, man. It was there to stay, so it was. Goin
nowhere.

Every cunt's jumpin about shoutin, Get the ambulance, get the
Polis, the doctor, any cunt at all. Any cunt.
Ye go loopy when somethin like that happens. Fuckin crack
right up. Fuckin panic stations. Ye sober up. Aye, ye go sober
as fuck.

Calm down, man. Relax. Don't fuckin panic.
Think. Ye've got to fuckin think. What're we gonni do, troops?
Fuck sake, look at the state of her. Can't leave her like that.
Look at her, man. Aw fuck, she's all dead an boaky an blue an
screwed up an twisted.
Can't leave her like that, man. No way.
Lift her up. Aye, c'mon, sit her up straight. Clean her up.
Dignity.

Mad Dog gets behind her. He slides his arms round her waist
just under her tits an locks his hands at the front.
Deep breath, man, deep breath. One two three, lift.

     GAAAAAAAUUUggggggggghhhhhhhhhheeeeeeee.

Nancy lets out a belcher. Aw, a fuckin beauty of a grunt so it
was. Aye, a big dull vinegar-stroke grunt.
Ye know the grunt ah'm talking about?
See when a burd's getting boned an she goes

    aw, aw, aw, baby aw, aw, ah'm comin ah'm comin

aw, awww ah ahh ah   aw, baby
guuuuffffffggfff?

Aye, well, see the bit where she goes guuuuufffffffgggffff at
the end?
It was like that.

Aaaaaarrrrrrgggghh, ya bastart, ya bastart bastart. Mad Dog
drops her like a shitey shovel an starts howlin like a wolf.

She's alive aw, man aw, man aw, man.

Aye, big Mad Dog's ecstatic, so he is. Starts jumpin for joy.
Jumpin about like an alky in an off licence. Starts callin her
darlin right in front of every cunt.

Aw, darlin yer alive yer alive, aw my fuck, yer alive.

But naw.
She's dead, man.
Dead.

The medic men in the green boiler suits show up. They just
strut in. Honest to fuck, man, ye want to have seen this. Just
strut in like the way ye walk into the boozer. Cool as fuck,
ah'm tellin ye.

She's dead, one of them goes. Definitely dead, he says. All the
tell-tale signs are there, like the blueness an the coldness an
the tongue hangin out. An she's also pissed her pants, he goes.

Pissed her pants? That goes for fuck-all, man. Pissed her pants?
Does it all the time.

Then the Polis show up. Need details.
They want to know all the particulars. Time of death an all
that shit. The Polis look at Mad Dog.

Aw, man, wait till ye hear this bit, aw, wait till ye fuckin hear this. Swear it, by the way, ah nearly died.
D'ye know what the Copper does? D'ye know what he fuckin does?
The big cunt goes an asks Mad Dog if he's the husban. Aye, honest to fuck, man.

Are you the husban? he says.

Aw, fuck me, man. Déja vu. Aye, remember? 'Hey mister, are you ma uncle?' Play it again, Sam. Same old story, only this time ye can't laugh, eh? Naw, ye can't, man. Come on for fuck sake. Respect.
Poor Nancy. Aw, Jesus, man. Poor wee Nancy. Dead as a dodo. Tell ye the saddest bit. Wait till ye hear this, by the way. Hey get the fuckin hankies out.
See the medic man ah was tellin ye about?
He starts describin Nancy into this wee tape machine.

WHITE FEMALE. FIVE FOOT SIX. SIX STONE
APPROX AGE FORTY-SEVEN, FORTY-EIGHT

Poor Nancy. She was only twenty-nine. Honest to fuck. Twenty-nine years young. Dead. Fuckin dead, man. Not even thirty. Naw. Never saw thirty summers. Just a wean so she was. Died without livin. Used an abused. Dead.
An ah'll tell ye another think that'll melt yer ticker. This'll break yer fuckin heart by the way.
Nancy had a mammy. Aye, a lovely wee mammy.
Saw her at the funeral.
We were all standin there. Standin round the grave. The Crazy Gang. Me, D, Chuck, Mad Dog an Sid.
Hangin our heads in shame. Shame.
It was a small turnout, man. Just a few people.

Aye, that's all there was. A few people, a few prayers.

So there we are, standin there like dirty big black crows round
a dead dog, a howlin wind drivin into our backs stingin the
nerves an chisellin into our bones, big pot-bellied clouds waitin
to open their bladders an piss down the necks of our misery.
The auld girl's all decked out in black.
Must be what? Seventy-five, eighty. Dead eyes spillin tiny tears
on a leather face.

Ma wean, she says. Ma wean.

Mad Dog's haunted.
Aw, my God forgive me. Cryin like a baby.

The words, ma wean ma wean, scream through his ears an bite
big chunks out his brain.
She was a wean. Nancy was once a wean. Newborn wean.
Aye, took her first steps an said her first words, man. Sat on
her daddy's knee an sang nursery rhymes. Played with dolls'
houses an wore pink ribbons an pigtails on her first day
at school. Had her first boyfriend. Had her first kiss behind
the sheds.
Where'd it all go wrong, man?
First kiss, first fag, first fuck. It's the fuckin people, so it is. It's
the people ye meet an the company ye keep. Ye get in with
the wrong crowd, man, that's all it takes. Downhill all the way.
D'y'know what ah'm sayin, man?
See the point of no return? Ye never see it, so ye don't. Ye
don't, ah'm tellin ye. Before ye know what's hit ye yer right
down the shit-hole without a fuckin shovel.
Meet yer first bastard drink yer first bottle of cheap wine an
do yer first gang-bang.
The party's over. Nancy's dead, man. Nancy's dead.

Who killed Nancy? You tell me.
Every fucker's guilty.
Holy Mother of God, pray for us sinners. NOW.

Goin nuts. Aye, the big guy was goin nuts, so he was.
She took a fast black cab. Her an the weans.
Her. She. The wife. Rose, that was her name. Did you know
that? Not a lot of people know that.
My sweet Rose, he would say. Swept her off her feet. Sweet
sixteen an never been kissed.

Me an you babe. Take on the world. That's a promise doll. Take
on the world. Make lovely babies. Baby boy like me baby girl
like you. Build a big bungalow, drive a big jeep, buy a fancy
flat in Spain. Just you an me babe, just you an me. Sky's the
limit. Promise.

Promises promises promises. Chopped up an shredded into
pieces, man. Fucked in the fire.
Aw, the poor weans. Sad wee faces sittin at the window.
Waitin. Waitin on Daddy. Daddy's takin us fishin, to the
pictures, to the park, to the sweetie shop.
Where's Daddy? Mammy, when's Daddy comin home?

Poor wee weans. Sittin, waitin, watchin. Watchin the clock
tick-tockin away.
Had it up to here, her an the weans. Offski. Took a fast black.
Rosie left a note.

Gone for ever. Never comin back. No choice. Got to go now for
sanity's sake. While there's still hope. Still a flicker. Leave
tonight or live an die here. Here in this shit-hole.

Dyin. Rosie's dyin, man. Broken heart.
Mad Dog breaks things. That's what he does by the way,

destroys everything he touches.
Broke sweet Rose. Crushed her. Crushed her tender petals.

Mad Dog's goin loco. Screamin bawlin headerin walls. Fuckin useless bastart. Mad Dog's in pain, so much pain, man. Aw, it hurts, the fuckin truth hurts. Can't stand the truth. Can't stand the man in the mirror.

His big head's gone, man, gone walkies, joggin, runnin, racin. Aye, Mad Dog's head's a turbo jet. A million miles an hour, the auld imagination, man. Goin haywire. Her, can't get her out his mind. He sees her in his crazy fuckin mind an she's all dolled up in the leather mini skirt stilettos fishnets n little black G-string. Aye, out there flauntin it. All the young team are like horny dogs round a bitch's arse. Ye know what it's like. Young team, see a thing at forty an they're hot knobbin it, man, droolin at the mouth. Aw, ya dirty bastarts yees.

Mad Dog's mind's a dungeon.

Chapter Fifteen.
Dog eat dog.

Mad Dog was losin the plot big-time. Becomin scarier by the minute. He would just bust out bubblin. Bubble like a baby, so he would. Just done it in the bog at first. Aye, at first he'd fuck off out of sight an come back with smudgy red eyes an greet about the smoke.

Aw, the smoke in this place would fuckin blind ye, he'd go. Some cunt open a window.

But then he'd stop carin, man. No more runnin to the lavvy. No more givin a fuck who saw him. Big man would just sit at the bar an break his heart.

No cunt would say a word. Not at the end up, anyway.

At first cunts would go up to him an seem all concerned. Tryin to get in the Dog's good books, so they were.

What's the matter, big guy? C'mon, cheer up, look on the bright side.

Next thing the big filla would give it bang bang bang bang. Aye, fuck ye.

Two upstairs two downstairs an the poor cunt'd be star-shaped. Tuppenny book shot.

At the end up, Mad Dog would sit bubblin an every cunt would just leave him.

It's the weans, he'd snivel. Aw, the poor fuckin weans, the weans need their auld man every laddie needs a Da. Every wean needs discipline. A father figure. A role model.

Aye, he had a point. Mad Dog had a point.

Mad Dog built a monster.
Taw. Just look at Taw. Taw's a perfect example. Taw turned out
to be a monster. A real fuckin monster.

No wonder. He'd been hearin all the lingo for yonks, man. Aye,
since he was knee-high to a gnome.
All the lingo, man, all the shit lingo. Dog eat dog. Look after
number one.

Aye, look after numo uno boy. Fuck them all. Aye, fuck them
before they fuck you. If any cunt hits ye, lift somethin an split
their fuckin head open. Don't greet ya wee bastart, naw,
better not greet or ye'll get somethin to greet about.

Aw, for fuck sake, man, poor Taw. Poor wee cunt, man. Hearin
it since he could hear.
Taw was brought up on all that shit. Weans remember, so they
do. Remember everythin. The bad old days. Taw remembers
the bad old days. Lyin in the cot bawlin the eyeballs out an the
shitty nappy wrapped round the neck. Aye, he used to lie
there greetin. Greet greet greet. Well that's what weans do,
innit? When there's somethin wrong, ye greet an yer mammy
comes an lifts ye an yer hugged into the sweet smell of warm
an tender boozum.
Rock-a-bye-bay-beee on the tree tops. There there, baby's OK,
Mammy's here shhhhh shhhhh.

Fuckin forget it, man. No chance. Not in Taw's house.
Taw hasn't a scoobi. Cuddles an kisses? Dunno what ye mean
mate.
Taw stopped greetin early doors. No point. He soon got the
message. Cry all night, baby. Cry till ye croak. Makes no odds.
Mammy's out the game. Mammy's lyin on a greasy chair with
the tits out an the heels behind her ears getting shafted an

givin whiskey lollypops to big hairy-arsed tarmen.
Cry all you like baby.

Aye, the wee man. Streetwise as fuck, so he was.
Mad Dog got him a start. He started with the tar squad, so he
did. Joined the Crazy Gang. Salesman. Taw was the salesman.

Ye want to have seen the wee man shiftin the gear.
He could sell shit to the sewerage works so he could. Aye, no
bother by the way. The wee cunt could head down to the auld
dung factory with a bucket of shite an come out with a nice
little earner.

You name it, yer man's shiftin it. There's fuck-all that can't be
sold. Fuck-all.

Shovels picks brushes rakes, there he was round the doors
givin it, Here you are sir, best of gear for your garden, just
what you're needin, knock-down prices, half the price of what
you'll pay in the shops an it's a home delivery as well, sir. Aye,
bring them to yer door so we do, none of this auld carry-on
havin to trail round B&Q with the missus lookin at all sorts
of shit.
Naw, naw, naw. Taw man brings it to yer door.

Hey, wait till ye hear this bit.
Ah remember him havin a slight problem gettin rid of the
picks. Ah mean, it's not every gardener that needs a pick is it?
Naw. So the auld picks weren't sellin like they should.

Fuck it, man, no problem. No problemo to the Taw filla. The
wee man just goes, Fuck ye, an whips the head off it. Ye know
the metal pointy bit? Just whips that bit off an throws it to
fuck. Ye know what happens next don't ye? Aye.
Roll up, roll up. Baseball bats for sale.

See? See what ah'm sayin? The bold Taw boy. Entrepreneur-extraordinaire. Arthur Daley eat yer heart out.
Wait an ah'll tell ye what else the wee cunt used to sell.
We had these screamin bright green luminous safety jackets that Hovis made ye wear.

Where's yer green jaiket? he'd go. Aye, put it on.

Mad Dog would do his nut at the big bastart.

Big bastart, he'd go. Fuckin safety-jacket, ma jacksie. What the fuck's safe about them, eh? How the fuck're ye safe? So if a big forty-ton lorry doin about ninety trundles you into the ground, do ye just jump back up? Is that what happens, eh? Aw fuck aye, man, no problem. Safe as houses, so ye are. Safe as houses as long as yer wearin yer auld super dooper safety-jacket. Aye, big fuckin artics just bounce off ye.

Taw was sellin the green jackets, man. Ah'm tellin ye by the way, the young team went mad for them. Fuckin absolutely mad for them. They all bounced about the raves with the auld fluorescent stripes glowin in the dark like some fuckin Star Wars free-for-all. Dance floors full of shiny skeletons.

ASSSEEEEEEEEEEEEEEEEEEEEEEEEEEEEEEEDDDD

Honest to fuck, man. Hot cakes. They were sellin like hot cakes. Fiver a time. Three for a tenner. Q'n up so they were. Cunts were Q'n up.
It was amazin the stuff he shifted. Stuff ye'd never think about.
Ear muffs. Taw was shiftin ear muffs, for fuck sake.
Wee foamy cone shaped things the size of fag tips. Place was polluted with them.
The invasion of the Mini Daleks.

Wait an ah'll tell ye how that came about.
No cunt wore them. No way, man. Looked like poison pishin
out yer ears, so it did. Aye, looked like yellow septic. Honest.
See from ten yards away, it looked like yer brains were pishin
out yer lug-hole. Fuck that, man. Every cunt walkin about with
yellow shit pissin out their ears! No chance.

What did Taw do? Aye. Got it in one.
Started puntin them.

Who the fuck would buy them? ah hear ye thinkin.
Wait an ah'll tell ye.
Cunts with teenage kids, man, that's who. Think about it.
Some young plooky-faced cunt gonni be a rock star an blastin
out the guitar riffs ten-a-fuckin-penny. Aye, the poor auld
maw an da can't get a wink. Well, Bob's yer auntie. Here, stick
these things in yer lugs an nighty night.

An then there's the poor cunts with the neighbours from hell.
Ye know the type ah mean? Never worked a day in their life
an have arse-rippin parties till four in the mornin seven nights
a week.

No problemo now, sir. Here ye go. Pop these in yer lug-holes.
Sweet dreams.

Aye, the bold Taw. The door-to-door saviour.

Here you are, sir. Wee cone-shaped ear muffs, comfy as ye like.
Don't even know they're there, so ye don't. Greatest thing
since flavoured condoms.
D'ye know how the ear muffs came about by the way? Wait an
ah'll tell ye. Industrial Deafness.
Every cunt in the tar game was struck deaf overnight.
Aye, every cunt was jumpin about goin, What? Eh?

What was that? What did ye say say?
All of a sudden not a cunt could hear a thing, man. Strange.
Every cunt an their auntie's deafer than big Bobo.
Tarmen from all over the world were comin out the skirtin
boards an jumpin on the bandwagon.
Done yer nut in at the end up. It was alright at first, so it was.
Aye, just a wee joke, man.

Have you got a deafy form?
What?
Where do you get them?
What?
Naw, seriously, ah'm wonderin where to get a form?
Eh?

Fuckin bastartin fuck cunt fuckin fuck fuck fuck fuck. Do yer
fuckin nut in, man. Every fucker takin it as serious as lumps on
yer bollocks.
An then all the heavy-duty story-toppin started.

Fuckin hell, some cunt would go. Nearly got knocked down
there, so ah did. Never heard that double-decker bus comin.

Tell ye a better one than that, somebody'd say.
D'ye know why ah was late this mornin? Missed ma train, so
ah did. Sittin on the platform readin the paper an didn't even
hear the fuckin thing comin into the station. Honest.

Aw, that's fuck-all, man.
Ah was sittin in the house last night an half the street were at
the door givin it, Turn that fuckin music down, ya cunt, the
buildins are startin to crack with the vibrations. Music? What
music? Didn't even know the radio was on, neither ah did.

So like ah say, every cunt's into it. Gettin a right few bob.

Aye, at the start it was no bother. The cunts were payin out
like a Las Vegas puggy.
Big bucks, man. Yer talkin big bucks.
Handin over money like a bullied schoolboy.
At first they were just askin a few questions.
They'd tell ye to stan over there with yer back to the wall.
What's yer name?
What's yer age? Can ye here me loud an clear or is it a bit
muffled?

Cunts were just standin there slingin it a deafy.
That was it so it was. That was all ye had to do. End of story,
man, the cheque's in the post. Two thousan smackeroos on its
way. Get the fuckin drinks up.

That went on for so long, so it did. An then it became tighten-
up-the-the-purse string time. They started gettin stricter.
Aye, they started usin wee gadgets. Wee electrodes on yer arm
that check the pulse rate an tell if there's a reaction. Tell if the
auld lugs are workin right or if yer just tellin porkies. Aye.
So Mad Dog gets a KB, so he does. Aye, knocked him back.
Offered him a job in fact. Honest. MI5 wanted to know if he
fancied bein a spy. Spyin on the Russians, listenin in on the
auld secrets, like. Aye, he could hear the cunts whisperin from
here, so he could. Mad Dog's ears are keener than a frosty
mornin. Big cunt can hear Christmas comin.
Knock back. End of story.
Naw. End of story, my arse.
Loophole. Mad Dog's lawyers found a loophole. This is where
the auld earplugs bit comes in. Compulsory. Yer earplugs were
supposed to be compulsory. See all yer Health an Safety shit?
See when they were hittin ye with all that, Where's yer green
jacket where's yer hard hat where's yer steel toe-tecters?

Well, that was just to cover their arses. Anythin goes wrong then, it's too bad. Tough titty. Ye've been told. They've told ye. They've covered their arses.

But no cunt ever mentioned ear muffs. Naw, they forgot to mention the fuckin ear muffs. Hadn't made it compulsory.

YEEEEEEEEEEEHHHHHHAAAAAAAHHHHHH

Aw, ya fuckin dancer, man, the cheque's in the post. Every cunt an any cunt's gettin paid out. Aye, payin ye the money whether yer deaf or not, so they were. It didn't matter a fuck. Ye weren't told. No cunt told ye. Yer hearin was put in danger through negligence. Negligence, man. Big Hovis had been negligent.

Hundreds of thousans of pounds it cost them. Aye, cost them a fuckin fortune.

We kept hearin noises round about that time. Aye, we kept hearin this screamin an howlin an all sorts of dull-leather-goin through-skin-an-crackin-against-bone noises.

D'ye know what it was by the way? Big Hovis gettin his arse booted all over the Town Hall. Well, as ye can imagine, after that they started gettin delivered by the lorry load. Aye, that's how the earplugs came about.

Honest to fuck, man, ah'm tellin ye, we were into everything bar a nun's knickers. Business empire. Aye, Mad Dog used to call it our little business empire.

Ye've got to expand, he would say.

Hey, listen, we were expandin like a whore's pussy in a ten-man gang bang. We were all sittin this day an the Taw filla came out with a beauty.

What does every fucker need?

Think think think.

Smoke alarms. Aye, in these Health an Safety-conscious days
everybody needs a fuckin smoke alarm.

Well, the wee entrepreneur extraordinaire Taw boy starts goin
round the doors. Aye, ye want to have heard the wee cunt
givin it the patter.

Eh, excuse me, madam, you don't happen to be interested in
saving yourself an your children from an absolutely horrible
death, by any chance?

The silent menace, madam, ah trust you've heard about the
silent menace?

Taw had done his homework. Aye, he dug up these pictures of
houses that had been burned to cinders. Aw, my fuck. Dunno
where he got these pictures. Pictures of weans with plastic
faces. Aye, weans with melted candlestick complexions.
It was the guilt-trip card. The Taw man played it from the
bottom of the pack.

What sort of person would put their beautiful children's lives
in jeopardy for the sake of a lousy fiver, he would say to
punters. Not you, madam, not you. I can tell you're not that
type. A loving caring parent's written all over your face,
madam. Without a shadow of a doubt. One can tell a mile off.

Aye, ye want to have heard this. The auld Taw boy was layin it
on thicker than the village idiot. Bring tears to a set of mole-
skins, so he would.

That's right, madam, five pounds is all it costs. That includes
free fitting. A fiver, madam, a lousy fiver. Wouldn't buy you
forty fags.

Taw was givin them all the patter about needin one in each

room too. Aye, one for each room. Ah mean, some of these big houses in the suburbs had ten an twelve rooms, so they did. No bother to the Taw. The wee cunt was doin knock down prices, special deals like, ye know?
Say a house had mibbee twelve rooms. Taw was doin the whole lot for fifty brick.

Fifty brick, man. Fifty brick for half an hours work.

> We are the Crazy Gang
> The Crazy Gang are we.

Sing up, troops, sing up. Aw my fuck, man, we were singin it. Singin it loud an clear. Happy days. Money flowin through our fingers like soft warm sand.
A golden flowin river.

But then one day it happened. The bubble burst, didn't it? Well, ye know what they say, don't ye? All good things come to an end. Every bubble goes pop, every bloomin red rose wilts dies an withers away.
See all yer Crazy Gang shit that we were singin about?
Fuckin forget it. Finished. Party's over, man. Finito.
Crazy Gang no more.

It was the council that caused it. Bastarts. All of a sudden they go all fuckin people safety-conscious don't they?
Some bright spark dreamin up a vote-catcher decides on freebies. Aye, they start givin out freebies, man, start givin the council tenants free fuckin smoke alarms as part of yer new lets-make-our-homes-a-safer-place-to-live campaign. The war against the silent menace.

Aye, freebies, man. Freebies.
Fuckin shower of bastarts.

So all of a sudden there's problems galore. Mucho problemos,
man.
See that fuckin business empire that ah was tellin ye about?
That golden flowin river runnin smooth an sweet an fillin up
the honey pot week in week out?
Well the level's startin to drop, so it is. Dy'know what
ah'm sayin?
Fuckin dryin up.
Aye, look, see last week's tide-mark? It's way up there.

Well ye can't let it happen can ye? Naw. Can't, can't, can't.
No way José, says the Taw boy. Ain't gonni happen, man. No
way back now.

Ye see, once you've had it good you adapt a certain taste for
things. Dy'know what ah'm sayin? A taste for a certain
lifestyle. Taw's had that taste an he ain't gonni let it go. Ain't
goin fuckin back, man.
Ah mean, if y've never had nothin ye miss nothin. But once
y've sucked on sirloin ye can't go back to mince, right?

Taw had vivid memories. Childhood memories. Days in the
playground. Ye know what kids are like, man? Cruel little
bastarts. Aye, cruel little cunts, so they are.
Taw can still hear the voices. Hauntin voices.

Look lads, the voices go, look at his trainers. Fuck sake, where
d'ye get the trainers, eh? What market? What jumble sale?
Aye, what part of Taiwan were yer trainers made, wee man?
An what about those joggers, eh? Ah saw yer daddy wearin
them last night doin the garden.
Aw naw, it couldn't've been, naw, that's right you haven't got
a daddy. Yer uncle mibbee? Aye, y've got plenty uncles. How,
many uncles have ye got wee man, eh? Aye, you're in the

Guinness Book of Records for havin the world's biggest
amount of uncles.

Taw remembers it. Remembers it all too well. The high-pitched
shreeeky laughter's like an icy sword slashin through his spine.
The Taw man ain't goin back to that. No way, man.
Won't let it happen.
Naw. Die first.
Fuck it, man. Drastic action time. Got to change the tactics. No
more softly softly approach. No more Mister Nice Guy.
An approach of the more sinister variety is what's needed now.
Time to squeeze the jugular.
Hey, check the face. Check Taw's face. It's a pure fuckin poker
number now.
Standin there with the auld deadpan look an that cold glassy
glare of his. Honest to fuck, ye should see the wee cunt's eyes
when they stare. Real frosty fuckers.

So he's out chappin away at doors an cunts are all startin to
give it, Naw, naw, the council says they're free. Aye, we've had
letters from the council sayin they're freebies, ye don't pay for
fuck all.

Well, the wee man just fixes them with the stare,doesn't he?
Starts layin it on the line.

Haw, listen hen, he goes, ye need these smoke alarms, right.
Aye, ye fuckin need these ones.
Now ye don't want no fuckin fires do ye?
Naw. Ah mean, look at those lovely kids of yours. Ye don't
want them getting all burnt to death. A fuckin horrible death,
so it is, gettin killed in a fire. D'ye know it's not the flames that
kills the weans? Naw, it's the smoke.
Can ye imagine that mucky black smoke sneakin right into yer

little babies' lungs, eh? They reckon the lucky ones don't feel a
thing if the smoke gets them first. But some poor cunts ain't so
lucky. Ye hear some horrendous stories about weans with their
flesh all bubblin an screamin for their mammy an no cunt can
get near them for the piercin heat an the deathly stench of
that burnin black smoke. For fuck sake man, can ye imagine
those screams? Haunt ye forever. Nearest thing to hell.
Fires? Horrible things fires. Never know how they can start.
Don't want any fires startin in YOUR house now. DO YE?

Aye, people's faces froze with fear when he punched out the
DO YE bit.
It was no question, man. Naw, no question. He was tellin them
fuckin straight.
Smoke alarms. Ye're buyin them.

Well, it's only a matter of time before some cunt sticks him,
innit? Aye, the Taw boy ends up getting lifted an banged up in
jail. The Polis pull him in. Want to ask him some questions.
They start hittin him with all this nicey-nicey shit. They want to
make a deal. They start tellin the Taw boy they know the score
about him, they know he's just a lad, just a youngster tryin to
make a few bob. Just a pawn in life's big fuck-you-before-you-
fuck-me-game.
Aye, just a fuckin foot-soldier. A message boy.
They tell him it's Mister Big they're after. Let's do a deal, they
tell Taw. Think about it, son. The Polis tell Taw to think it over.
Mad Dog made a monster. Poor Taw boy. Just a wean. Had to
grow up fast, man. No childhood. Just memories of gang
bangs an bevvy sessions.
Mad men gang bangin Nancy.
His poor wee maw.
Taw thinks about his maw. Nancy. Nancy's dead.

Taw has visions. Flashbacks. Hairy-arsed he-men. Bare-arsed
tarmen. Taw thinks about it. Thinks long an hard. Thinks about
Mad Dog. Where is he now, eh? Big fuckin he-man. Bare-arsed
tarman. Aye, words. Words ring out so true. Come back to
haunt ye sometimes. Taw remembers all the shit talk.
Fuck em all. Fuck em all bar Nancy. Numero uno. Dog eat dog
Aye, exactly.
Taw thinks long an hard. Fuck em all. Numero uno. Look after
numero uno.

Fuckin big Mad Dog. Big bastart. Dog eat dog.

Chapter Sixteen.
The fanny an the Charlie Nash.

Mad Dog's in jail. Dropped his guard.
Aye, big Mad Dog. Big fuckin always-watch-yer-ass-trust-no-cunt-look-after-number-one Mad Dog. Dropped the auld guard, man. Aye, the auld guard went down quicker than a whore's head on a hard-on.
Aw fuck, man, ye'd never believe the way it happened.
Honest. Weird so it was.

Listen to this.

Down at Nicky's Bar.
We're shootin pool right? There's me, Mad Dog, Crazy D an a shower of other crazy cunts. We're all swiggin back the swally givin the auld pool table pelters an splashin the cash like cunts with no pockets.
Well, as tarmen do seven nights a week, eh?

Big Nick, man, Great big cunt. Me an yer man go back yonks.
Pure money-makin machine, so he is. Absolutely minted.
Loves the auld cash, man. Aye, loves the auld Charlie Nash.
Take his granny a square go for a fiver so he would.
Money mad.
So as ye can imagine he's well chuffed to see all the Crazy Gang givin his boozer big licks.
Big cunt just sees all these fuckin pound signs with the tarry boots on sittin round his pool table.
What's he like, eh? He's like the auld Scrooge filla, only worse.
Ah'm tellin ye, he'd make yer man Ebenezer seem like wee Andy Carnegie.

So ye can imagine how shocked ah was when he strolls over an shakes ma han. Here, he says, get all the lads a drink.

Ah open ma hand an it's full of these wee washers. Aye, the big cunt had went an filled ma hand with fuckin washers. Ya bastart. Ya big fly bastart. Should've known. Fuckin fly big cunt.

Ah'm just about to go like that an call him all the big fly bastarts under the sun when he goes, Naw, naw, naw, they're kosher mate, honest to fuck, ah use them as tokens for the puggy. Worth a pound a piece. The big lassie behind the bar knows the script.

Aw, fuck me. Sound, big man. Cheers.

Well, it was all fair enough up to that point. But it was after that it all started to go pure fuckin radio rental.

See the big lassie behind the bar that he was talking about? Well, the big Dog filla just happens to be in the process of teasin the panties off her big wobbly arse. Aye, he's up there givin it his auld faithful. Ye know the one ah'm talkin about don't ye? Aye, the auld three-young-team-under-the-bridge yarn. Fuckin usual. So anyway, there he is jumpin up in the air an headerin this cunt an givin the next one the auld bang bang bang bang two upstairs two downstairs routine an then doin the auld bit of Morris dancin on the guy that's lyin on the deck's head. Aye, ye know the script don't ye? Y've heard it all before.
But the thing about the auld Mad Dog is, the big man's got built-in radar. This wee red eye comes out the corner of his head goin

doo doodoo doo doo doo doo doo doo doo doo doo doo doo

It zooms right in on the auld transaction between me an Nicky.

Aye, honest to fuck. No bother to the Mad Dog filla to focus
on two things at once, man. Especially if it involves his
two very most favourite things. The auld bit fanny an the
Charlie Nash.
Ah'm tellin ye, two things at once is a doddle, an absolute
pish case.

Fuck sake, man, give me somethin hard to do for fuck sake,
he'd say.

So he's seen it no bother, but he carries on kiddin on he hasn't.

An then all of a sudden right out the blue he breaks from his
Morris dancin an zooms right over an starts givin it, Aw, how
ye fixed buddy how're ye fixed? Listen by the way, ah'm on to
an absolute cert here, honest. Swear to fuck, man, it's absolutely bitin the leg off her, so it is, she's fuckin gaggin for it.
Swear it. Absolutely gaggin for yer man's doaber. Tell ye what
ye could do mate, bung me some of that dosh ye got an ah'll
buy a wee round up for yees all. Know what ah mean? Bound
to impress the pants off her if ah do that, eh? Aw, what a big
fuckin rich handsome cunt, she'll be sayin to herself. Won't be
able to resist the Dog after that, so she won't. No chance, ah'm
tellin yees.

Well ye know what he's like when he's horned up, don't ye?
Pure fuckin hyper-head.

Ah bung the tokens into his hand an go to explain the script to
him but he just goes whoooooosh.
Off like that wee cartoon cunt on the telly that makes the auld
meeep meeeep noises. Aye, away he went, man. Big fuckin
dust jets sprayin out his arse.

Fuck it. Too late. Ah decide to leave the big cunt to get on with it.
Aye, payback time for all the wind-ups the big fucker's played on us down the years, we're all sayin to ourselves.

Check him out, man, what's he like, eh?

My name's Mr Flash what the fuck's yours?

Look at the big cunt. Mad Dog doin what only he would get away with. Show-boatin so much he's gettin seasick. Aye, honest. Check him out, man. Turnin pure yellow.
Ready to start boakin any minute.

He goes like that to the big thing: OK babes, decorate the mahogany. Full round of drinks for the troops. What yees havin, lads, eh? OK, OK, same again then. Alright, that'll be six half pints of lager, two vodkas, two whiskies an three glasses of buck. No problemo, man. An oh, by the way, have one yerself darlin. Aw, c'mon now, ah must insist. No, no, no, ah won't take no for an answer, neither ah will. It's only money after all, only old pieces of dirty paper. No time for these tight-fisted fuckers. Money's for spendin. Just love bein allowed to spoil a lady, so ah do.
What's that? Brandy an babycham? Aw, go'n yersell sweet-heart, not a problem. In fact ah'll tell ye what, make it a double. No, no, no, ah must insist.

Everthin's workin a wee treat. The big thing's poutin like a pair of pink pussy lips. The king-size keks are half way down her arse. Well impressed.

Now listen to this bit. Big picture time.
Mad Dog digs deep. Dips the big han into the sky rocket.
It actually crossed our mind at this bit to tell him.

Na, fuck it.
So he digs in, right? Opens his big han.

Freeze frame. Mad Dog's face is like a portrait on the wall.

Every fucker freezes. Mouths hangin open. Eyes gapin.
Ah'm tellin ye, by the way, there must've been at least forty
sets of beady eyes starin down Mad Dog's throat due to the
big fuckin song an dance he had made about buyin a few
swallies.

Mad Dog looks down at his han. Looks up. Looks down. Looks
across at all us cunts. Looks back at his han. Then looks up at
the big thing.
There she is, the big dame standin there with the han out, the
long painted fingernails pointin deep into Mad Dog's mind.
That'll be fourteen pound fifty, big boy.

What the fuck, man? What the fuck? What's he gonni do, eh?
What's he gonni fuckin well do?

Choices. Mad Dog's got choices.

Put it on the slate? Na can't do that, man. No way José. Look a
right fuckin tit-head after all that pish talk about not bein able
to stan tight-fisted cunts.

Can ye just put it on the slate darling?
Na, no chance.
He could always pull a Mad Dog special an point over at one
of us an say, He's payin.
Aye, the big bastart used to do that all the time. Sometimes he
used to order up a full round of drinks an stick it on some
other cunt's slate.

But naw. Can't do that this time. Can't. Just can't.

We're all watchin. Aye, we're all watchin an lappin it up big time. What ye gonni do now Dog, eh? What ye gonni do now, ya big cunt?
Payback time, big style.
Every dog has its day. Ain't that right, eh?

He takes one long look up at big thing.
Big hot thing. Hot an horny, spicy an ripe. Eyelashes flickerin like interference on yer telly. An then he takes one last look over at us. By this time we're all rollin about the place pishin ourselves laughin. Aye, pishin ourselves good style. Big cunt can't do nothin either. Just stans there rooted to the spot. Stans there pure shocked, so he does. Aye, pure shocked an stunned, man. Mad Dog doesn't know what to do.

But listen. Ah saw Mad Dog's look changin. Changin from what-the-fuck's-the-script-here-lads-what's-goin-on? to right-now-that'll-fuckin-do-ya-bastarts-enough's-enough.

An ah'll tell ye, better still, he was lookin straight down the eyeballs of yours truly. Aye, starin hard an bad at yer man here. Fuckin scary stuff. Fun time over, bro. Time to call it a halt. Time to put him out his misery. Aye, c'mon, big guy, just a laugh an a joke. Just a wee wind-up.
So we're just about to tell him he's been fucked up the arse by the biggest wind-up this century an tell him the score about the washers bein worth a quid each an that he's no chance of shaggin the big thing now cos every dude an their dog knows that he's a big tappin bastart an that he'll never be able to show face in here again without takin a pure fuckin beamer. Aye, we're just about to do that when

FUCK YE, MAN
HEY PRESTO!

Talkin about pullin a rabbit out yer arsehole, wait till ye
hear this.

The big bastart just went, Fuck ye.
An then he dipped into the inside pocket an pulled out a wad
of notes as thick as snot in a wean's nose.
Honest to fuck, man. All ye seen was all these sets of beady
eyes blinkin like two thousan flash-lit cameras takin yer
picture.
Big Mad Dog. Big fly bastart rides again, man. We had him
too. Had him by the shorties an the big fucker went an
escaped. Couldn't believe it, man. Couldn't. No cunt could.
Even Harry Houdini would've phoned the fuckin Fire Brigade
to cut him out of that mess.
Not Mad Dog but. Na, no chance.
The big man just stuck the chest out, peeled off a couple of
notes, paid for the drinks an then went straight back into the
auld knockin-fuck-out-of-three-cunts under the bridge routine
without breakin sweat.
Cool as fuck, eh?

Hey, but listen. It turned out to be his downfall.
The big filla broke the golden rule.

Never trust no cunt, he used to say. They're all out to get us.
They're watchin us, men. Always keep the chin tucked in an
the elbows tight together. Keep the auld guard up. Always
keep yer guard up.

Aye, Mad Dog dropped his guard.
It was Mad Dog's downfall.
Boozers? Ye know what boozers are like, don't ye? Aye, the
auld walls have ears eyes an mouths, man. Full of jealous
cunts. Jolly green giants. Green-eyed monsters. Cunts that

don't like to see anybody getting a wee turn. Ye know what
they're like, eh? Gobby fuckers. Stick ye in in a minute.
Bad news spreads like syphilis. This was bad news, man. Bad
tom-toms.

The Polis were waitin to pounce. Fraud Squad.
They went an raided Mad Dog's house.
Ye want to have seen this. They found wads of notes that
would've choked a pack of donkeys.
An ah'll tell ye another thing, ye want to have seen the gear.
Picks shovels rakes wheel barrows brushes gloves overalls
green jackets donkey jackets water-proof jackets earmuffs
hard-hats goggles wellies. You name it, Mad Dog had it.
Honest to fuck, by the way. Ye want to have seen this.
MAD DOG'S HARDWARE STORE.
Listen, B&Q was on a three-day week.

Mad Dog was fucked. Fucked fucked an well fucked. Up the
creek. Down the swanny. Stuck down the shitter with no bog
roll.

The Polis Station stunk of pish, so it did. Looked like an auld
folks' home. A trail of auld fogies the length of big Chuck's
tadger were all standin there waitin to give evidence. Bring on
the hard-luck stories.
The newspapers are churnin them out too.

Bogus workmen. Cowboys. Extortionists. Hairy Monster.
Mr Big.
Lookin for a big hairy gap-toothed cunt.
ID Parade.
Aw, for fuck sake. Mad Dog's got as much chance as a choirboy
at a priests' piss-up. Sittin duck, so he is. Stans out like a
steamin-hot dog turd on virgin snow.

That's him, that's him, that's him.

Who shopped Mad Dog?
Who stuck him in, man?
Who would do that?
Eh?

Did Mad Dog have enemies?
Fuck sake. Do cows do big watery turds in fields?

Chapter Seventeen.
Nil by mouth.

Mad Dog's in jail. Done, man. Dubbed up.
Big Mad Dog. Dog eat dog. Who said that?

Mad Dog's dead, so he is. Well, not quite dead. Dyin. Mad
Dog's dyin. Aye, the big guy's up in hospital. Fuck sake, man.
Where? What hospital? What for? Bammycain maybe?

What's he up to, we're all thinking. Probably at the madam.
Ye know what he's like, the Mad Dog? Fuckin Shakespearian
actor. Equity card. Like ah said before, Mad Dog would put
Robert De Niro on the dole queue.
Aye, fakin it. Fakin it like a happily married woman. Lookin for
a wee cushy night in a nice soft bed with nice soft sheets
gettin pampered rotten by a lovely white angel. Lyin pullin his
puddin at her wee tight arse.

Naw. Naw, that's not the case.
Mad Dog's in a bad way. Critical. Ah'm tellin ye. Givin death's
door's letterbox a right good clatter, so he is.
Bleedin. Bleedin all over the shop. Internal, external, you
fuckin name it, the big dude's bleedin it.
Aw, my fuck, man what happened? What the fuck happened?

This is what happened.

Ulcer. Mad Dog's had ulcers since he was six.
His ulcer's actin up like fuck. Mad Dog gets whipped up to
Casualty screamin the face off every cunt.
So they get him sedated an bedded down for the night. Gonni
operate in the mornin.

Just a simple op, man. No worries by the way. Naw. A stroll in the park. Child's play.

No worries my fuckin arse, by the way. Turns out there's big elephant's-baws-size worries.
Tragedy in the theatre. A fuck-up on the slab, on the op table. A slice with the knife an Mad Dog exploded. Aye, his insides exploded, so they did.

Turns out Mad Dog had a bellyful. A belly full of grub. Ham eggs bacon sausages, the lot. Big greasy fry-up lyin in his belly.

Hows that?
Nil by mouth!
Should've been a sign, eh? Fuckin easy peezy, man. Plain an simple.

Naw. Is it fuck. It's plain an simple fuck-all. Let's face it, in Mad Dog's life nothing ever is.
Ye see, the nil by mouth sign was there alright. Aye, big green fucker of a sign right above his bed. Screamin out at ye. Can't miss it, man. Can't fuckin well miss it.

How did it go wrong then? How did the big filla scran up? What happened? What the fuck happened?

Ah'll tell ye what happened.
What happened was this.
The previous night Mad Dog was lyin in bed sweatin like a serial rapist. For fuck sake, man. Can't breath, can't breath. Sweat's pishin out him. Cookin.
Big man's claustrophobic as fuck. Walls start closin in on him. Fuckin heebi jeebi's. Got to move. Got to get near a window. Fresh air, fresh air, need to get some fresh air.
Gonni die, man.

The cunt in the next bed gets a dunt.

Haw, cunt, shift, move. Swap beds.

Mad Dog makes him swap beds.
That's better. That's the game. Mad Dog's in his glory, so he is.
Cool breeze. Floatin on a cool breeze. Floatin off to baw baw
lan. Out like a light in no time.
Tiny little zzzzzzzzzzzzzzzzzzzzzzz's flyin out the window.

So the next morning Mad Dog gets the wakey-wakey call.
Aye, in comes the wee nurse. Wee fat lassie in a grey tunic.
Auxiliary. Pishy pay. Doesn't give a fuck. Real crabbit lookin
cunt. Just started her shift an still half sleepin.
So she shuffles in, clocks the nil by mouth sign an keeps
walkin. Aye, walks up to the next bed, so she does. The one
next to the window. No sign on it. No nil by mouth sign. OK,
she says. No problems. Here's yer breakfast big yin.
She hans the breakfast to the guy in the bed, right?
An guess who's in the bed? Yip. Got it in one. There he is, man,
the bold Mad Dog sittin up in bed slobberin at the mouth like
a big fuckin ravenous prairie dog.

Ye know what Mad Dog's like, don't ye? Sore belly or no sore
belly, the big man would eat a cow's arse raw.
Munch munch munch. Wolfs it down in seconds.
Yummy yummy.
Aye, he horses it down the hatch an jumps back into his
own bed.

Haw, up ye get ya cunt, up. That's ma bed. Get yerself to fuck.
Shift.

Easy peezy, man. Back into the nil by mouth bed an no cunt's
none the wiser.

Naw, not until they got him to the theatre an cut him open, that is.

Mad Dog's insides hit the ceilin, so they did. Erupted. Honest to fuck, man. Big Vesuvius style eruptions. Blood guts, the lot. Artexed the walls.

Mad Dog's a dead man. Dyin. Lyin there dyin, stitched up like a tramp's trousers, surrounded by doctors an nurses. Ain't gonni make it, man. Ain't much hope.
Pray for him. Every fucker pray for him. They're all there. Priest. Wee maw. The missus. Prayin. Splashin holy water. Holy Mary Mother of God.

Mad Dog's wired to the moon, so he is. Check him out, man. What's he like? Fuckin wires everywhere. Big man looks like the inside of a telly.

The wee telly on the wall's long high-pitched beeeeps go shorter n sharper.
The needle's pointy squiggles draw longer n smoother.

He's driftin. The big man's driftin.

Floatin away.

   Floatin off with flyin angels.

        Floatin.

Off,
   off to the big stretch of tarmac in the sky.

Peter's at the Pearly Gates.

How's it goin Pedro ma man? Mad Dog'll say.
Lovely big driveway ye've got there. Could do ye a good deal, by the way.

Some other books published by **Luath** Press

Me and Ma Gal
Des Dillon
ISBN 1 84282 054 0
PB £5.99

This sensitive story of boyhood friendship is told with irrepressible verve.

Me an Gal showed each other what to do all the time, we were good pals that way an all. We shared everthin. You'd think we would never be parted. If you never had to get married an that I really think that me an Gal'd be pals for ever. That's not to say that we never fought. Man we had some great fights so we did. The two of us could fight just about the same but I was a wee bit better than him on account of ma knowin how to kill people without a gun an all that stuff that I never showed him.

Dillon captures the essence of childhood. He explores the themes of lost innocence, fear and death, writing with subtlety and empathy.

'Spot on.' BIG ISSUE IN SCOTLAND

'Reminded me of Twain and Kerouac... a story told with wonderful verve, immediacy and warmth.'
EDWIN MORGAN

'Ripe with humour and poignant vignettes of boyhood...'
SCOTLAND ON SUNDAY

Me and Ma Gal was winner of the 2003 World Book Day *We Are What We Read* poll.

Six Black Candles
Des Dillon
ISBN 1 84282 053 2
PB £6.99

'Where's Stacie Gracie's head?'
... sharing space with the sweetcorn and two-for-one lemon meringue pies ... in the freezer.

Caroline's husband abandons her (bad move) for Stacie Gracie, his assistant at the meat counter, and incurs more wrath than he anticipated. Caroline, her five sisters, mother and granny, all with a penchant for witchery, invoke the lethal spell of the Six Black Candles. A natural reaction to the break up of a marriage?

The spell does kill. You only have to look at the evidence. Mess with these sisters, or Maw or Oul Mary and they might do the Six Black Candles on you. But will Caroline's home ever be at peace for long enough to do the spell and will Caroline really let them do it?

Set in present day Irish Catholic Coatbridge, *Six Black Candles* is bound together by the power of traditional storytelling and the strength of female familial relationships. Bubbling under the cauldron of superstition, witchcraft and religion is the heat of revenge; and the love and venom of sisterhood.

'Hilarious.' THE MIRROR

'An exciting, entertaining read... just buy it.' THE BIG ISSUE

Driftnet
Lin Anderson
ISBN 1 84282 034 6
PB £ 9.99

Introducing forensic scientist Dr Rhona MacLeod...

A teenager is found strangled and mutilated in a Glasgow flat.

Leaving her warm bed and lover in the middle of the night to take forensic samples from the body, Rhona MacLeod immediately pervceives a likeness between herself and the dead boy and is tortured by the thought that he might be the son she gave up for adoption seventeen years before.

Amidst the turmoil of her own love life and consumed by guilt from her past, Rhona sets out to find both the boy's killer and her own son. But the powerful men who use the Internet to trawl for vulnerable boys have nothing to lose and everything to gain by Rhona MacLeod's death.

A strong new player on the crime novel scene, Lin Anderson skilfully interweaves themes of betrayal, violence and guilt. In forensic investigator Rhona MacLeod she has created a complex character who will have readers coming back for more.

'Lin Anderson has a rare gift. She is one of the few able to convey urban and rural Scotland with equal truth... Compelling, vivid stuff. I couldn't put it put it down.'
ANNE MACLEOD, author of *The Dark Ship*.

But n Ben A-Go-Go
Matthew Fitt
ISBN 1 84282 041 1
PB £6.99

The year is 2090. Global flooding has left most of Scotland under water. The descendants of those who survived God's Flood live in a community of floating island parishes, known collectively as Port. Port's citizens live in mortal fear of Senga, a supervirus whose victims are kept in a giant hospital warehouse in sealed capsules called Kists. Paolo Broon is a low-ranking cyberjanny. His life-partner, Nadia, lies forgotten and alone in Omega Kist 624 in the Rigo Imbeki Medical Center. When he receives an unexpected message from his radge criminal father to meet him at But n Ben A-Go-Go, Paolo's life is changed forever. Set in a distinctly unbonnie future-Scotland, the novel's dangerous atmosphere and psychologically-malkied characters weave a tale that both chills and intrigues. In *But n Ben A-Go-Go* Matthew Fitt takes the allegedly dead language of Scots and energises it with a narrative that crackles and fizzes with life.

'I recommend an entertaining and ground-breaking book.' EDWIN MORGAN

'the last man who tried anything like this was Hugh MacDiarmid' MICHAEL FRY

'Bursting with sly humour, staggeringly imaginative, exploding with Uzi-blazing action.' GREGOR STEELE

Milk Treading
Nick Smith
ISBN 1 84282 037 0
PB £6.99

Life isn't easy for Julius Kyle, a jaded crime hack with the Post. When he wakes up on a sand barge with his head full of grit he knows things have to change. But how fast they'll change he doesn't guess until his best friend Mick jumps to his death off a fifty foot bridge outside the Post's window. Worst of all, he's a cat. That means keeping himself scrupulously clean, defending his territory and battling an addiction to milk. He lives in Bast, a sprawling city of alleyways and claw-shaped towers… join Julius as he prowls deep into the crooked underworld of Bast, contending with political intrigue, territorial disputes and dog-burglars, murder, mystery and mayhem.

'This is certainly the only cat-centred political thriller that I've read and it has a weird charm, not to mention considerable humour…' AL KENNEDY

'A trip into a darkly surreal and richly-realized feline-canine world.' ELLEN GALFORD

'Intriguing, different and well-paced' EVELYN HOOD

'*Milk Treading* is equal parts *Watership Down*, *Animal Farm*, and *The Big Sleep*. A novel of class struggle, political intrigue and good old-fashioned murder and intrigue. And, oh yeah, all the characters are either cats or dogs.' TOD GOLDBERG, LAS VEGAS MERCURY

The Road Dance
John MacKay
ISBN 1 84282 037 0
PB £6.99

The bond between a mother and her child is the strongest in the natural world. So why would a young woman, dreaming of America, throw her newborn baby into the waves of the wild Atlantic ocean?

Life in the Scottish Hebrides can be harsh – 'The Edge of the World' some call it.

For Kirsty MacLeod, the love of Murdo promises a new life away from the scrape of the land and the suppression of the church. But the Great War looms and the villages hold a grand Road Dance to send their young men off to battle. As the dancers swirl and sup, Kirsty is overpowered and raped by an unknown assailant. She hides her dark secret, fearful of what it will mean for her and the baby she is carrying. Only the embittered doctor, a man with a cold wife and a colder bed, suspects.

On a fateful day of surging seas and swelling pain Kirsty learns that her love will never be back. Now she must make her choice and it is no choice at all. And the hunt for the baby's mother and his killer become one and the same.

'[MacKay] has captured time, place and atmosphere superbly… a very good debut.' MEG HENDERSON

'Powerful, shocking, heartbreaking…' DAILY MAIL

FICTION

Outlandish Affairs: An Anthology of Amorous Encounters
Edited and introduced by Evan Rosenthal and Amanda Robinson
ISBN 1 84282 055 9 PB £9.99

The Fundamentals of New Caledonia
David Nicol
ISBN 0 946487 93 6 HB £16.99

The Strage Case of RL Stevenson
Richard Woodhead
ISBN 0 946487 86 3 HB £16.99

POETRY

Tartan and Turban
Bashabi Fraser
ISBN1 84282 044 3 PB £8.99

Drink the Green Fairy
Brian Whittingham
ISBN 1 84282 020 6 PB £8.99

The Ruba'iyat of Omar Khayyam, in Scots
Rab Wilson
ISBN 1 84282 046 X PB £8.99

Picking Brambles and Other Poems
Des Dillon
ISBN 1 84282 021 4 PB £6.99

Kate o Shanter's Tale and other poems
Matthew Fitt
ISBN 1 84282 028 1 PB £6.99 (book)
ISBN 1 84282 043 5 £9.99 (audio CD)

Talking with Tongues
Brian Finch
ISBN 1 84282 006 0 PB £8.99

Immortal Memories
John Cairney
ISBN 1 84282 009 5 HB £20.00

Men and Beasts: Wild Men and Tame Animals
Valerie Gillies and Rebecca Marr
ISBN 0 946487 928 PB £15.00

Madame Fifi's Farewell
Gerry Cambridge
ISBN 1 84282 005 2 PB £8.99

Scots Poems to be Read Aloud
Introduced by Stuart McHardy
ISBN 0 946487 81 2 PB £5.00

Poems to be Read Aloud
Introduced by Tom Atkinson
ISBN 0 946487 006 PB £5.00

Bad Ass Raindrop
Kokumo Rocks
ISBN 1 84292 018 4 PB £6.99

Sex, Death & Football
Alistair Findlay
ISBN 1 84282 022 2 PB £6.99

The Whisky Muse: Scotch Whisky in Poem and Song
Introduced by Robin Laing
ISBN 1 84282 041 9 PB £7.99

THE QUEST FOR

The Quest for Robert Louis Stevenson
John Cairney
ISBN 0 946487 87 1 HB £16.99

The Quest for the Nine Maidens
Stuart McHardy
ISBN 0 946487 66 9 HB £16.99

The Quest for the Original Horse Whisperers
Russell Lyon
ISBN 1 84282 020 6 HB £16.99

The Quest for the Celtic Key
Karen Ralls-MacLeod and Ian Robertson
ISBN 1 84282 031 1 PB £8.99

The Quest for Arthur
Stuart McHardy
ISBN 1 84282 012 5 HB £16.99

FOLKLORE

The Supernatural Highlands
Francis Thompson
ISBN 0 946487 31 6 PB £8.99

Luath Press Limited

committed to publishing well written books worth reading

LUATH PRESS takes its name from Robert Burns, whose little collie Luath (*Gael.*, swift or nimble) tripped up Jean Armour at a wedding and gave him the chance to speak to the woman who was to be his wife and the abiding love of his life. Burns called one of *The Twa Dogs* Luath after Cuchullin's hunting dog in *Ossian's Fingal*. Luath Press was established in 1981 in the heart of Burns country, and is now based a few steps up the road from Burns' first lodgings on Edinburgh's Royal Mile. Luath offers you distinctive writing with a hint of unexpected pleasures.

Most bookshops in the UK, the US, Canada, Australia, New Zealand and parts of Europe, either carry our books in stock or can order them for you. To order direct from us, please send a £sterling cheque, postal order, international money order or your credit card details (number, address of cardholder and expiry date) to us at the address below. Please add post and packing as follows: UK – £1.00 per delivery address; overseas surface mail – £2.50 per delivery address; overseas airmail – £3.50 for the first book to each delivery address, plus £1.00 for each additional book by airmail to the same address. If your order is a gift, we will happily enclose your card or message at no extra charge.

Luath Press Limited
543/2 Castlehill
The Royal Mile
Edinburgh EH1 2ND
Scotland
Telephone: 0131 225 4326 (24 hours)
Fax: 0131 225 4324
email: gavin.macdougall@luath. co.uk
Website: www. luath.co.uk